HOW TO MARRY A MATADOR

By
Ginny Baird

Published by
Winter Wedding Press

Copyright 2012
Ginny Baird
Trade Paperback
ISBN 978-0-9851235-8-1

All Rights Reserved
No portions of this work may be reproduced without
express permission of the author.
Characters in this book are fiction and figments of the
author's imagination.

Edited by Linda Ingmanson
Cover by Darleen Dixon

About the Author

From the time that she could talk, romance author Ginny Baird was making up stories, much to the delight -- and consternation -- of her family and friends. By grade school, she'd turned that inclination into a talent, whereby her teacher allowed her to write and produce plays, rather than write boring book reports. Ginny continued writing throughout college, where she contributed articles to her literary campus weekly, then later pursued a career managing international projects with the US State Department.

Ginny's held an assortment of jobs, including school teacher, freelance fashion model, and greeting card writer, and has published more than twelve works of fiction and optioned nine screenplays. She's additionally published short stories, nonfiction and poetry, and admits to being a true romantic at heart.

Ginny is an award-winning writer the author of several bestselling romantic comedies, including novellas in her Holiday Brides Series. She's a member of Romance Writers of America (RWA), the RWA Published Authors Network (PAN), and the RWA Published Authors Special Interest Chapter (PASIC).

Ginny lives with her family in Tidewater, Virginia. When she's not writing, Ginny enjoys cooking, biking and just about any word game, including crossword puzzles and Scrabble. She loves hearing from her readers by email at GinnyBairdRomance@gmail.com and can also be found online at http://www.ginnybairdromance.com.

HOW TO MARRY A MATADOR

Fernando sighed, worry lines creasing his brow. "You're terribly angry with me, aren't you?"

"It takes two to tango, Fernando. I'm not saying all of this is your fault. I played a part in what happened yesterday too."

He turned toward her with a penetrating look. "That's what I don't understand. Why did you?"

Jess felt a lurch of emotion as he dissected her with his earnest green gaze. "I...don't know."

He leaned toward her with a husky whisper. "Oh, but I think you do."

He drew nearer, his mouth hovering over hers. Jess cursed herself for so badly wanting his kiss. His kisses had been so tantalizing last night, they'd made her lose all sense of reason. And it wasn't just the way he'd held her. When he'd looked deep in her eyes and said that one thing, she'd inexplicably believed him as she had no man before.

"Why did you?"

Fernando reached out and cupped her chin in his hand. "Because, querida, when I saw you standing there in that garden, with that beautiful smile on your lips, I knew with a certainty that I'd have to claim them. That I wouldn't rest until I made you mine."

"It was a simple sexual attraction."

"There was nothing simple about it," he said, brushing his lips to hers.

Jess closed her eyes as her heart stilled. She couldn't let herself do this, but she couldn't stop herself either. His masculine scent washed over her as she felt his palm press into the small of her back.

*"Jessica," he said, resting his forehead on hers.
"When I tell you the truth about this morning, I don't want
you to believe that anything last night was a lie." And then
to prove it, he kissed her deeply, with a skill and a passion
that made her lose grip of her wine, sending the contents of
her cup sloshing sideways.*

*"Your sister's riding pants," she said, nearly
breathless.*

"They'll wash," he said, tenderly stroking her thigh.

"Fernando," Jess gasped, pulling back. "We can't."

*He studied her a thoughtful moment as she gazed at
him wide-eyed.*

*"Then we won't," he said with a quick peck on her
lips.*

*She shivered involuntarily in spite of herself. This man
had a way of completely undoing her.*

*"We'll have a little something to eat first." He pulled
several small bundles from his bag, along with a small
knife and a cutting board.*

"While we talk?"

*"Of course," he said, handing her a napkin for her
slacks. "Then afterwards, I'll let you decide."*

"Decide what?"

Fernando shot her a sexy grin as he refilled her wine.

"Whether or not I'm the husband of your dreams."

Chapter One

Jess rolled over into a wall of steel. She opened her eyes, encountering a strong, masculine shoulder. Hoofbeats echoed outside to the sound of *ándale, ándale, vámanos*! Her gaze panned the spread of his broad, olive chest, graced with charcoal hair matching the wavy array on his head. Impossibly perfect cheekbones offset a patrician nose. No Renaissance sculptor could have crafted a finer face. Jess's mind whirled, recalling the evening of wild flamenco dancing and sangria. *This slumbering specimen can't be, but he is!*

She gingerly lifted the sheet and peered beneath it with a gasp.

"Good morning, *princesa*," he said, emerald eyes upon her.

Jess pinched the duvet to her chest, her face on fire. "Fernando."

He turned toward her, covers gaping. "I trust you slept well," he said, trailing a finger down her arm. Little shivers raced up her spine, then plummeted in a dead heat toward her tailbone. He brought warm lips to her shoulder, gracing it with a kiss. "I also hope," he said, his Spanish accent trilling, "you meant what you said last night."

Panic tore through her as she desperately tried to recall. Gracefully, he filled in the blank. "That you were happy to be my wife." *Wife? Did he just say wife?*

Fernando tenderly peeled back the duvet, admiring the curve of her hip beneath a satiny sheer nighty. His palm centered on the small of her back as he angled his ruggedly handsome face toward hers. "And you took pains to prove it," he said in a husky rasp, pressing her lower region toward his vivid response.

Jess pushed back with a start and pinched her forearm, certain she would wake up. He lazily pulled himself partially upright on one elbow, resting his head in his hand.

Jess stared, dumbfounded, while Fernando lifted his brow and waited.

"What…is the meaning of this?" she asked, covering herself primly.

"Don Fernando!" a voice called through the screenless window in gruff Castilian. "You still riding this morning?"

Fernando shot Jess a questioning look. She quickly shook her head.

"Not today, Pedrito!" he called back in English. "We're sorry to have troubled you!"

"We?" Jess asked, her voice escaping as a whisper.

"You insisted I take you riding. Don't you recall? It was the second thing you wished to do as my new wife."

Jess felt the heat bolt to her temples and chin. Suddenly, it all came back to her. The late night at the bodega, Fernando's unexpected and utterly passionate kiss, their unanticipated encounter with that Catholic priest… Jess swallowed hard past the burn in her throat.

She'd come to Madrid on an acquisitions merger but had married a matador instead.

Fernando watched as the beautiful woman leapt from the bed, snatching the duvet with her. Honey-blonde hair cascaded past delicate shoulders as she suddenly averted brilliant blue eyes.

"You should cover yourself," she insisted.

"But it seems my new wife has taken the covers."

"And stop saying that!" she cried with an indignant pout.

"What? That you're my wife? I do apologize," he said, sitting upright and scooting to the edge of the bed. "Perhaps it's better if I call you my bride."

Jess instinctively stepped back. "Now, Fernando," she began with a wave of her finger. "You know as well as I do that—if anything happened last night—it wasn't supposed to."

He noticed she was trying not to peek at him but was failing in her efforts. He took this as encouragement to drop his feet to the floor and face her outright, sporting his full glory.

"Is that what you Americans mean by, *Take me back to your bed, you beast. I'm yours?*"

She gasped audibly. "I said that?" she asked with unmasked horror.

Taking pity on the woman, Fernando covered his lap with a feather pillow. "You can look now," he said with a sigh.

She steadied her chin, settling her gaze on the window. "How do I know I can trust you?"

"I guess you don't," he replied. "But I'm inviting you to take the chance."

Slowly, she turned her eyes toward his. They were an amazing shade of blue, aquamarine, really. Fernando felt as if he could swim in them forever. He recalled thinking that yesterday evening, after a few too many pitchers of sangria and a splendidly expensive bottle of cava. Perhaps he'd gotten carried away in asking her to be his bride. But after the flamenco show and the kiss by the fountain, their surprise encounter with his old friend Father Domingo had seemed nothing less than a direct sign from God.

"Where are my clothes?" she asked, color sweeping the bridge of her nose.

Fernando pointed to the armoire beside the door leading to the well-appointed bathroom.

"I suppose the shower's in there?" she asked, angling her head in that direction.

"There are fresh towels on the stand behind the claw-foot tub," he said.

Her cheeks flamed red. Perhaps she did remember everything.

"Fine, thank you," she said hoarsely, sidestepping her way across the floor, the hem of the duvet trailing over inlaid tile.

"Would you like something to eat?" he called after her. "I can have Consuelo bring up breakfast."

She skittered into the bathroom, partially closing the door. "Just coffee!" she called before shutting it with a bang.

Fernando sat upright with a start and tossed aside the pillow.

"Consuelo?" he said into the intercom by the bed, pressing its button.

"*¿Sí, señor?*" a kindly older voice asked from the kitchen.

"*Dos café con leche, por favor.*"

"*Two*, Don Fernando?"

While it had come as surprise, Fernando didn't precisely view his marriage as a mistake. In fact, given the timeline imposed by his grandfather for inheriting his fortune, this little twist of fate just might prove fortuitous.

"*Sí, dos.* And, if you will, place a pretty, fresh rose on the tray. I have something happy to tell you."

Jess let the water run hot, hitting her full in the face. Any second now, she was going to wake up in her apartment in Brooklyn, her best friend Evie calling her on the phone about some recent catastrophe that had occurred… Jess's mind raced, putting pieces of the puzzle together.

Fernando Garcia de la Vega's emerging telecommunications firm had been a long-term associate of her multinational corporation headquartered in New York. While Jess wasn't super tech-savvy, she knew how money worked. Trained in the banking industry, she'd earned her stripes by helping arrange the takeover of United National Savings & Loan's domestic division by InTrust Corp. While she'd really been the second in that job, her magnanimous superior had given her the bulk of the credit. The offer to head up the foreign acquisitions office at Global Financial Telecom had come just two weeks later. She'd accepted the post with a mixture of joy and trepidation. There she was at twenty-eight, and—according to everyone else—finally making her way. Inwardly, she feared she'd bitten off more than she could chew. She'd never handled such a large responsibility alone. What if she made a disaster of it all and failed everybody in the process?

While Global Financial had started as a bank, it quickly expanded into the lucrative computing field, piloting the first purse-size, all-purpose computer. With computing and telecommunications becoming so intricately linked, interest in other types of personal electronic devices followed. So far, Jess had done a reasonable job, impressing her stern, middle-aged boss Madeline with her string of unlikely successes. She didn't know how her mergers had always come through, but it appeared as if she had an invisible good luck charm buried somewhere deep in her pocket. Each time she got assigned to something new, Jess silently feared her luck would run out. Now, it appeared it finally had.

Jess shut off the water and reached for a towel, her gaze panning toward the bedroom. How could she have let herself get swept away? So what if Fernando was gorgeous, intelligent, and had an accent to die for? That was no reason to go shedding her clothes and getting married! Jess cinched the towel around herself, realizing she had that in the wrong order. The marriage part had come before the hopping into bed. But why had she done it? She wasn't that old-fashioned, for heaven's sake. Sleeping with a man after a few too many sangrias and a momentary lapse in judgment was one thing. Saying "I do" under the arch of an orange tree in the courtyard of some small church whose name she couldn't pronounce was something else entirely.

Jess warmed at the memory of Fernando kissing her by the main plaza's fountain, sweetly at first—and then with the passion of a parched man determined to drink her in. Her face flashed hot as she further recalled Fernando's skilled, masculine touch once he'd brought her back to his lair. The ranch was breathtaking in its desolate beauty, rows of olive trees threaded by moonlight, a faraway vineyard trailing over burnt hills.

She hadn't even known he'd come from a family of matadors or had once worked as a bullfighter himself. These were stories he told to few people, he'd assured her with a tender caress before leading her up the stairs. While the townsfolk of La Esperanza del Corazón viewed him as a hero, in Madrid Fernando was just a successful businessman. Neither the family he came from nor the world he'd left behind had any bearing on his corporate potential. So he'd shuttered away his past, vowing to reserve its unveiling only for those special parties with whom he might share a future. He'd led her to his bed then, saying that their impromptu marriage had been a blessing, something he'd never wish undone—no matter how she might think of him tomorrow. And, when he'd offered to show her the scar that tore from his upper left thigh to his navel, she'd found it impossible to say no.

Jess moistened a washcloth from a nearby stand with cool water and pressed it to her chest. Fine trickles slid south, gliding into her cleavage.

Okay, so she'd admit it. Ever since they'd first met six months ago, she'd been reduced to a handful of putty each time he'd given her that deep, expressive look with those impossibly unnerving eyes. Still, she'd steeled herself against him, understanding that when he was being flirty, it was likely in the interest of his own financial gain. That was just what Fernando was: untrustworthy. Which was precisely why she had no reason to trust him now. Fernando was up to something with this marriage bit, and Jess was determined to learn what. But first, she needed to find an Internet connection and research Spanish marriage laws. Surely, things couldn't be as bad as they seemed.

Fernando hummed a love song and strategically angled the tray, rearranging its bud vase for maybe the tenth time. *Ridiculous*, he told himself. It was only a flower. But none could be as sweet as the delicate rose that had opened up for him last night. Fernando would be a liar to say he hadn't wanted her—*ached for her*—for months on end. He'd never seen a face so lovely or known a mind so sharp. Hers was such an intoxicating combination, he might even have married her without the wine.

Though he'd secretly imagined laying her in his bed at least a dozen times, he'd never envisioned the sheer ecstasy of actually being with her. She was so sweet yet tough, like a tiger in the wild. And her kisses were the nearest thing to heaven. If the bright Andalusian sun hadn't awakened him from his slumber, he might have thought he'd fantasized the whole thing. He'd stirred early to find a sleeping angel beside him, then had quickly shut his eyes, lest she evaporate like an enchanted dream. The next thing he knew, she was moving beside him, carefully peering under the sheet to ensure he possessed the correct…accoutrements needed to fulfill his husbandly duties. Fernando sighed, thinking he'd be glad to perform those again and at any time his willing wife was ready.

He stared toward the bathroom, noting the shower had stopped. This might not be the most standard way to begin a union, but it certainly couldn't be the worst. Fernando was sure that Jessica would agree—once she got over the shock.

Jess exited the bathroom with a combative air and made a beeline for the armoire.

"Coffee this morning?" he asked, smiling sweetly over the rim of a cup. He extended it in her direction with the calm demeanor of a waiter at an upscale restaurant. She noted his lower region was still covered by a large feather pillow, the musculature of his tanned upper thighs exposed to the morning breeze fluttering in through the window. His toned olive chest sported richly dark hair which tapered in perfect symmetry down the line of his taut abs and plummeted toward the breakfast tray balanced on his lap.

She hesitated a moment, then decided she'd think better after the java. "Fernando," she said, cinching the oversized towel around her and cautiously inching forward. "You and I have something to discuss."

He handed her the coffee, then nonchalantly dipped a bit of pastry in his own cup. "I never discuss business before breakfast," he said, slurping loudly. "Mmm. This *pan dulce* is delicious. You ought to try it."

"I'm not hungry," she said, steadying the cup in her hands.

"Ah yes, that's right," he replied with a knowing wave of his finger. "Fairly well satisfied last night. Eh?"

Jess felt her face flash hot as his impish green eyes danced with mirth. "I don't find any of this very amusing."

"I'm sorry, Jessica," he said sadly. "I suppose I was a fool, hoping that you'd be just as excited about this as I."

She took a slow sip of coffee, studying him all the while. "You claim to be a fool, Fernando. But you're certainly not fooling me."

He raised his brow, perplexed.

"Come on," she said. "Give. What's in this for you?"

"My new wife has cut me to the quick," he said, bringing a hand to his chest.

"Argh!" She spun toward the armoire, clumsily setting down her cup down on a nearby stand. Porcelain clattered against itself with the effort.

"You're getting too upset about this," he said.

"I...don't...think...so," she said as she furiously tugged her clothes from huge wooden hangers, then strode toward the bathroom.

"*Querida*," Fernando said softly, "please wait."

She stopped walking, her pulse pounding. It picked up as she felt him behind her, his warmth drawing near. Instinct said that Fernando hadn't carried the pillow—or anything else—with him. "Perhaps it was...impetuous, unexpected," he said, palms pressed to her bare upper arms. Goose bumps rose on her flesh as the heat of his breath warmed her neck. "But you can't completely believe it was wrong."

But it was wrong, worse than wrong. Marrying Fernando had to be the most terrible decision she'd ever made!

"I have a boyfriend," she said, the lie escaping as a whisper.

"What a shame." Palms slid down her arms as Fernando brought his lips to her shoulder. "How do you think he'll take the news?"

Jess gasped, fighting her automatic feminine response. Nipples hardened beneath terrycloth, and she ached to turn toward him. Being made love to by a strong, confident man like Fernando was nothing short of heaven. The truth was that she and Allen had broken up weeks ago, and the physical relationship they'd shared hadn't even come close. Still, the illusion of another man was good, maybe the best thing she had at the moment. Until her head cleared, Jess needed every ounce of ammunition against Fernando's manly advances that she could muster.

"He'll be outraged," she said, pulling her mound of clothing in tighter.

"He must love you desperately."

Jess pursed her lips, fighting the fire in her eyes. The fact was, she didn't know whether Allen had loved her or not. Just as with her past two boyfriends, he'd never broached the topic—and she'd never yearned to discuss it.

"I don't do love," she said hoarsely, making an effort to step away.

Fernando tightened his grip and spun her toward him. "Everybody *does* love," he said with an earnest look. "Sooner or later."

Jess blinked back the moisture in her eyes. "Not this girl."

Fernando released her, his brow creasing. He'd never seen a woman at once so fragile and strong. There was a sorrow in her eyes that made him want to weep for, and with, her. He wondered how long she'd contained it, keeping that sadness to herself.

"I'll just be a minute," she said, turning away.

Fernando watched her leave, thinking this presented more of a challenge than he'd imagined. Then again, if ever there was a man who knew how to rise to the occasion, it was him.

"Take all the time that you need," he said as she exited the room.

Jessica emerged fully dressed ten minutes later. "As soon as we return to Madrid," she said, "we're getting this thing annulled."

She was beautiful today, smartly polished in a short white dress. He'd be proud to introduce her, if only she'd trade that frown on her lips for one of those winning smiles.

"Annulled?" Fernando questioned, glancing sideways as he straightened the collar of his polo shirt in the mirror. "Don't you think that's a little rash?"

"No, Fernando. Rash is getting married to a business colleague after too much sangria. Rash is *not* doing the sensible thing the next morning."

Jess didn't know how she'd let herself get talked into it, but she had. Right down to signing that statement of Proof of Freedom to Marry, endorsed by Father Domingo's brother-in-law, the retired American Consul, whose powers of persuasion were still apparently in force.

"But we weren't married in Madrid," he noted astutely.

Jess considered this a moment, realizing he was right. The marriage had to be annulled right here. But first, she needed to learn precisely where that was. "Where are we?"

"In La Esperanza del Corazón, remember? Place of my birth."

Yes, it all came stampeding back to her, like a trillion *toros* on the run. "Of course I recall."

"Everything...?" he asked, suggestively lifting an eyebrow.

Jess shook her head in agitation. She was not going to let him do this, have her remembering all the *wrong* things. "I was tipsy…animated, okay? Foolishly and hopelessly in love with life!"

He beheld her wistfully. "Yes, it was lovely."

Jess fought for the words. "It was reckless," she countered. "That woman you were with last night wasn't me."

"No? Who was it?"

"Someone else." She huffed, trying to imagine how she'd explain this to her mother. Jess had never gotten so much as a B on a report card. Now here she was, failing life. "My evil twin."

He laughed out loud. "You're a Gemini?"

"What?"

"The zodiac sign."

She was puzzled by this turn in the conversation. "What do constellations have to do with anything?"

"Perhaps we're written in the stars," he said, a sly smile on his lips.

Jess pressed her palms to her temples, thinking hard. Before she told her mother, she'd call Evie; that was what she'd do. Evie would help her straighten things out. If Jess could fix things fast, maybe her mom wouldn't even have to know.

"I'm a Taurus, if it matters."

"I might have guessed."

"What's that's supposed to mean?"

"The Taurus and the toreador? And you tell me there's no fate?"

She set her jaw, her eyes boring into his. "Fernando Garcia de la Vega, I want you to show me to an Internet connection this minute!"

"That might be a bit complicated. You see, out here *en el campo*, we have limited…" His voice fell off as he took in her increasingly enraged form. It was one thing to lightheartedly provoke someone. But at this very moment, Fernando sensed he was putting himself in mortal danger. "Okay, all right," he said, flagging a hand in her direction. "I can see when I'm not wanted."

His expression took a downcast turn that almost made her feel sorry for him. The truth was, Jess had wanted him, *wanted him in the worst way*, which was precisely what had gotten her into this mess! She pulled her cell from her purse and checked it for the tenth time this morning. She still wasn't picking up service. Just how far from civilization were they?

Fernando gestured grandly toward the door that led downstairs. He unlocked it, then held it open. "Fair's fair, Jessica. After all, no one's holding you prisoner in an ivory tower. So, here's what we'll do. You and I will have a civilized talk about everything that happened last night. Then, if you're still determined to get out of this marriage, I won't stop you. I'm far too proud a man to hold a woman against her will."

Jess's heart skipped a beat as something raw and unanticipated burned inside her. She couldn't say whether it was relief she felt or something more akin to disappointment. Why, oh why did his admission that he was fine in letting her go resonate with something so utterly painful in her core?

Jess shook off the odd déjà vu and met his gaze, his green eyes playing the soft serenade of a Spanish guitar. Jess caught her breath, lost for a moment in their music.

"I also believe," he said slowly, "that sometimes things happen for a reason. And often that reason is far too grand for us to originally understand."

But Jess didn't want to think about reasons or fate or star-crossed lovers—or any of that other nonsense Evie so ardently believed in but that she'd never been able to wrap her own head around. Jess was a practical person who saw the world for what it was. The fact that she'd long ago stopped believing in fairy tales had only worked to her benefit.

"The only thing I need to understand," she said, "is why you persist in saying this…accident of nature…was somehow preordained. "

He massaged his temples, apparently growing exasperated. "I already said I'll explain everything."

"Good," she said, stepping past him. "At last, you're talking sensibly."

Jess hurried down the stairs, desperate to get away. He smelled of sandalwood soap and lime, and the aroma awakened her memory of his showering kisses last night. The sooner she got herself out of this mistake of an arrangement, the better. And it better be before nightfall, lest she find herself tempted to leap back into that manly matador's bed.

"I've never been accused of being unreasonable," he said, trailing after her. "But I am known for keeping my commitments."

Jess halted in her tracks, fearing this was going somewhere. Somewhere that was going to land dangerously close to further confounding her emotions.

He captured her in his gaze, stilling her heart for a fraction of a second. Somehow, when he looked at her, it was as if he could see into her depths and behold her every weakness. And yet, his gaze soothed her, smoothing old hurts in tender ways. Warmth surged in her cheeks as he descended the steps two at a time, then gently cupped her face in his hands.

"And I *always* honor my commitments," he said, his voice a husky rasp.

Her pulse beat wildly, and for a second, she feared he would kiss her. Next, she was terribly afraid he might not.

"Most especially," he continued with an enigmatic smile, "to my mother."

Chapter Two

Jess couldn't believe she was having lunch with Fernando's mother. Everything was totally out of control. Señora Garcia de la Vega took a slow sip of wine, surveying the American seated before her. "Tell me again, dear," she asked, the sweetness of her tone slightly acerbic, "how is it that you know my Fernando?"

Fernando dabbed his mouth with a napkin, then set the cloth aside. "We met in Madrid. I explained the whole thing to you this morning."

"Perhaps," his mother said with a tilt of her chin. "But I'd like to hear the story from the young lady herself."

That would be great, if only Jess could recall the tale she was supposed to tell. She had no clue what Fernando had said to his mother earlier. All she knew was that Fernando had asked her to *"play along with things at lunch."* He promised her an Internet connection later, along with a cell signal in range so she could call Evie. Boy, would Evie have a field day with this. She was forever on Jess's case for being too stringent and unerring. Eve was the carefree one who made mistakes. Now, here Jess sat in the middle of some matador's ranch—and the global communications magnate didn't even have Wi-Fi! Things were positively prehistoric in La Esperanza del Corazón, and Jess had the feeling she was dining with a carnivore.

Mrs. Garcia de la Vega's deep brown eyes settled on hers as she carefully spooned cold gazpacho soup to her lips. Fernando's mother had to be in her late fifties but was beautiful still, fine wisps of gray just making themselves visible in her coiled-up hair.

Fernando reached across the table and squeezed Jess's hand, lending encouragement. "Just tell her how we met, *querida.* All the business deals and such." He lifted her hand to give the back of it a firm kiss, and Jess's resolve wilted. She was not seriously interested in Fernando in the least. They had chemistry—nothing more. And she resented the trappings of this little charade confusing her.

Jess withdrew her hand from his grip and massaged it with the one in her lap. "Yes, that's right," she politely told Mrs. Garcia de la Vega. "It was business. All business. Strictly business from the start." She shot Fernando a stern look to remind him their business here was nearly done.

"And your business is…?" the older woman prompted.

"Telecommunications, just like mine," Fernando interjected.

"The young woman speaks just fine for herself," his mother quipped, annoyed.

Jess uncrossed her legs under the table and sat up a little straighter in her chair. "The name of my firm is Global Financial Telecom. We're headquartered in New York, and I'm in charge of international acquisitions."

"Like my son, for example," Señora Garcia de la Vega said flatly.

A breeze ruffled across the tabletop, sending the fresh-flower centerpiece fluttering. While Jess normally loved dining outdoors, the chill hovering above them on this balmy afternoon was unmistakable.

"I came here on an acquisitions merger, it's true. Involving your son's *company*, Señora Garcia de la Vega. Fernando knew about… What I mean is, this was all arranged in advance. There were no surprises."

"Except for one," Fernando added with a wink.

A tension in her gut told her she was about to get broadsided. "Which one was that?"

"Why, you know, my love. That little unexpected package."

Jess felt the blood drain from her face. "Package?"

"Special delivery, *mi amor.* Our bundle of joy." Fernando scooted his chair against hers so he could drape his arm around her shoulder. "Mamá," he said, addressing his mother sincerely. "Jessica and I have known each other for months now. I've come to respect her not just as a business colleague but as a woman as well. A beautiful, sensuous woman that any man would be proud to call his—"

"Is there a restroom downstairs?" Jess asked, abruptly pushing back from the table and breaking Fernando's embrace. She stood unsteadily, glancing helplessly about the patio. Oddly, she felt more trapped in this beautifully arranged open space than in any cage.

"Past the kitchen," Mrs. Garcia de la Vega stated, her quizzical gaze on her son.

Fernando shrugged at his mom as Jess stood from her chair. "It's the baby."

"*Baby?*" The joint chorus was so loud neither Jess nor Mrs. Garcia de la Vega could be sure whose shriek registered the loudest.

Jess stared at Fernando and blinked hard, her wobbling knees forcing her back in her chair. "*That's too high a telecommunications price tag,*" she hissed under her breath.

"Consuelo!" Señora Garcia de la Vega cried desperately toward the house. "More water, please!"

Jess didn't know what game Fernando was playing, but she refused to be party to it. "Excuse me," she said, gathering her strength and standing again. "Mrs. Garcia de la Vega, thanks for a lovely meal, but it's time I head back to Madrid."

"Madrid?" Fernando and his mother parroted together.

"Yes, Fernando. Madrid. That's where I have an apartment—with an included Internet connection."

Mrs. Garcia de la Vega set aside her empty water glass. "We have an Internet connection."

Jess raised an accusatory eyebrow at Fernando. "Here?"

"Naturally," his mother continued. "Premium satellite. What else would you expect?"

What else would she expect, indeed? Nothing more than Fernando's continued conniving. The man didn't have an honest bone in his body!

"But Jessica," he began, pleading, "our arrangements. You and I should talk...alone."

"I think that's a very good idea," his mother said grimly. "This situation sounds serious. It is not one you settle in haste."

Fernando stood with a gallant air and took Jessica by the elbow. "This way, *querida.* We wouldn't want a woman in your condition taxing her nerves." Then he called back over his shoulder, "I'll see to it she calms down, Mamá."

As viciously as she could, Jess stomped her three-inch heel into Fernando's loafer.

"Ouch!"

"Son?" Mrs. Garcia de la Vega inquired as they slipped out the door.

"It's nothing. I just felt a sudden...twinge," he said, leading Jess from the room.

"Of guilt, I hope," Jess spewed under her breath.

"All right, Fernando," Jess whispered as Consuelo whisked by them, carting a chilled bottle of water. "What precisely was going on in there?"

Fernando raked his fingers through his hair, then addressed her with a strained expression. "The truth?"

"That would be a nice start."

"Okay, I'll tell you, but not here."

"Not here? Then where?"

Consuelo passed back by them, and Fernando called after her. "Consuelo, if you please, ask Don Pedrito to saddle up two horses."

Jess stared at him aghast. "First I'm pregnant; next I'm riding?"

"My mother rode until she was full term."

"Oh! That's what happened to you! Too many prenatal bumps to the noggin!"

"You *can* ride?" he asked.

She set her hand on her hip. "I was raised in a saddle."

"That settles it."

"*Gracias*, Consuelo," he said to the housekeeper, who studied them agape. Consuelo backed away, clearly not wanting to miss one moment of the action.

"What's all the shouting about?" Señora Garcia de la Vega called from outside.

Fernando pressed his palms together in a prayer position. "Please, dear Jessica, I'm begging you—for only a few more hours of your time. The rest of your life…whatever you opt to do with the information…those choices are yours."

Mrs. Garcia de la Vega stood in her spacious kitchen sternly appraising her son. "Are you sure you should take a woman in her condition riding? She's an American, you know, on the soft side."

"She's as healthy as a horse. Kickboxes, even. I'm sure she'll be fine."

"Kicks boxes, eh?" his mother asked. "And then what will she beat up next? Your heart, more than likely."

"No, Mamá, you misunderstand. It's an exercise."

His mother frowned, fine lines creasing her brow.

"Well, I hope she leaves kicking behind once she's a mother. It doesn't sound dignified and surely won't prove any sort of example—"

He fondly patted his mother's cheek. "I'll put her on Valencia, okay? She's as gentle as a lamb, and too old to trot too fast."

"We need to talk about this, Fernando. In detail."

"I know," he said, briefly holding her gaze, "but not yet."

"This has all happened so quickly. I didn't even know you were dating!"

"We more or less skipped over that part."

Señora Garcia de la Vega inhaled a sharp breath and narrowed her gaze. "Does this have something to do with your birthday?" She leaned into the center island as Fernando packed libations for his trip. Some noncarbonated water and a bottle of a regional Rioja. Almost as an afterthought, he tucked a wedge of Manchego cheese and a small hard roll in his satchel.

"I'm sorry," he asked blithely, "did you say something?"

She stood with her arms akimbo, lording over her kitchen. The moment Consuelo had sensed the ensuing fireworks, she'd made herself scarce.

Señora Garcia de la Vega disapprovingly shook her head. "You're forgetting the almonds. And, oh yes, the olives."

"*Gracias.* They slipped my mind."

She huffed as he stuffed small portions of these in his bag as well. "So?" she asked. "Are you going on a picnic or running away?" Since he'd been eight years old, the latter had crossed Fernando's mind more than a dozen times. Yet he would never leave her. When his father had died at forty-nine, Fernando had been left manning the ranch. While he'd grown older and had moved to Madrid, his heart remained in La Esperanza del Corazón. He would always take care of his mother. She'd been his source of strength and had granted him the freedom to follow his dreams, even when they included—for a time—dabbling in the one profession she'd prayed to God he'd never pursue.

"We won't be gone long," he said, buttoning up his satchel. "Back by nightfall, *vale*?"

She paused for a thoughtful moment, seeming to soften just a little. "Fernando," she said, "are you sure you're doing the right thing? Is this girl really the one?"

He pensively eyed his mother, knowing she wished only to protect him.

"The situation is…complicated," he said truthfully, without giving too much away.

"Love is always complicated," she admitted with resignation in her eyes.

"Yes, Mamá,*"* he said, kissing her on the forehead. "It is."

"I still don't think this is a good idea for the baby!" she called after him. "I was an experienced horsewoman, you know!"

He turned back with a gentle smile. "If she shows any signs of trouble, we'll abandon the horses immediately. Jessica's in top form, and it's still very early. I can assure you with my word as your son, I would never take my new bride riding if I felt that our child was in danger."

Chapter Three

Jess gripped the satellite phone with white knuckles. "He's a liar and a cheat, and I don't know *how* I let myself get talked into this!"

Evie's calm voice resonated from the other side of the Atlantic. "Now, if you'd just take a deep breath and calm down, maybe I'd be able to understand you. Inhale, come on."

Jess imagined Evie was twisting up her hair, as she did when taking on her consultant role. Evie's fiery red tresses fell in ringlets to her shoulders. She had a habit of twisting them into a French knot and securing it with any handy implement. Even a chopstick or a pencil would do. Jess had always envied that ability, as her own stick-straight hair wouldn't even hold a barrette.

Jess took a deep breath, then let it out slowly.

"Better?"

"Are we on speakerphone?" Jess asked.

"Nobody's here. Out for the three-martini lunch." Evie worked in a small yet prestigious publishing firm where publicity deals were forever being cut. As an assistant, she practically ran the place but still barely got paid. Jess was secretly ashamed to earn so much more than her, knowing that Evie worked just as hard. Jess didn't feel nearly as smart or savvy as everyone thought she was. She owed her early success to a series of lucky breaks. If things had broken differently, it could just as easily have been her sitting in her old college roommate's chair.

"Well, I'd appreciate you taking it off, just the same."

Evie's reply came back without the previous echo effect. "Okay, so tell me again, because I know I didn't hear you clearly. It sounded almost like you'd said you'd gotten married!" She affected a laugh.

Jess's heart lurched in her chest. It *did* sound absurd, and she knew it. Especially for her. Jess winced, hearing her voice come out as a squeak. "It's true, Evie. Oh my God."

"*What?*"

Jess bit into her knuckle, stopping her knee-jerk reaction at the first flash of pain. Her pulse was racing, and her head pounded. As bad this already was, somehow it sounded worse admitting it to her best friend. "I did it, Evie. Just last night. I married a matador."

Evie's tone was shrill with disbelief. "How did you do that?"

Jess grimaced. "It was a mistake."

Evie huffed into her mouthpiece. "No, Jess, a *mistake* is missing your connection at the airport, forgetting to pack extra panties! A mistake is *not* marrying a matador!" She paused a beat, then began slowly. "I know what this is. It's a joke, isn't it? Ha ha! Right?"

Jess stared down at the naked spot on her ring finger. As soon as there was time, he'd told her, he'd buy her a big, beautiful engagement ring—and a wedding band to match. Didn't matter to him that they'd never technically been engaged.

"Jess…" Evie queried. "The silence is scaring me."

"He's not really a matador," Jess said, blinking hard. "I mean, not anymore. It's more like the family business."

"So what's this guy do?"

"He's in telecommunications."

"Hold the phone. Wait just one New York second. This couldn't possibly be…? Is it Fernando we're talking about?"

Jess felt her face flash hot.

"But you hate the guy!"

"That's just what I was saying!"

"No. You said you'd married him."

"That too."

"Hoo boy."

"Yep."

"So, what did you do? Fly to the Spanish version of Vegas?"

"More like stepped into a time warp."

"I don't understand."

"La Esperanza del Corazón, some little Spanish town near Seville."

Jess could imagine Evie massaging her forehead. While Evie often got into trouble, she very rarely got stressed. Stressing was Jess's department. "When did this happen?"

"Just last night."

"Oh, good, then it's a fresh mistake. Go out and get it undone."

"I plan to," Jess said with more resolve than she felt. "Just as soon as everything here opens back up."

"What's wrong with today?"

"It's Sunday, Eve. And tomorrow is some sort of saint day. It will be Tuesday before we can get things straightened out."

"Did you sleep with him?"

Jess hesitated a moment too long.

"Maybe a little."

"A little?"

"Okay, it was a lot. Quite a lot. Four times, to be exact."

"That's some Latin lover."

Jess sighed, reliving the heat of Fernando's caress trailing down the length of her spine.

"That good, eh?"

"I didn't say that."

"You didn't have to!"

Jess heard footsteps on the stairs. "Look Evie, I've got to run. Fernando's taking me riding."

"Not on a bull, I hope!"

"Horses, Evie," she said in hushed tones. "He's promised to explain the whole thing."

"Which thing?"

"Why he wants to keep this sham of a marriage going."

"This sounds dangerous, Jess."

"He's not dangerous, I swear. In fact, he's a very devoted son."

"*You met his mother?*"

"And she thinks I'm pregnant."

"Jess!"

She heard him approach the door and rap soundly.

"Is my new bride ready to ride?"

"Oh my God, is that him? Love the accent."

"I'll call you later," Jess whispered. "As soon as I know more!"

"Wait! Don't—"

But Jess had already pressed End Call and opened the door.

Fernando smiled at her sweetly, a bulging satchel slung over his shoulder. "I'm glad to see my sister's riding clothes fit you so well."

Her face flushed as he gave her an appreciative perusal. The fact was, they were a bit snug, but Jess had managed to struggle into them.

"What will you tell your mother about taking a woman in my condition riding?"

"I already told her what I'll now promise you." He leveled her a look with his deep green eyes, and Jess once again had that tumbling sensation. "That I would never, ever put you in danger."

Jess caught her breath, wondering for a panicked second if he'd overheard her phone conversation.

Fernando brought a hand to her face and gently stroked her cheek. "You do believe that, *querida*?"

Jess felt her heart thunder in response.

In spite of herself, she did. She was actually starting to fear she'd too easily believe just about anything Fernando told her. She was glad they were going outdoors and far from this room and its host of heated memories.

"After you," he said, gallantly stepping aside and letting her pass.

Eve pulled the ballpoint pen from her hair and anxiously thumped its cap against her desktop. *Married to a matador!* How could the normally sensible Jessica have let herself get talked into that? What was more concerning still was that she actually seemed to be considering staying in that hasty marriage. Eve turned toward her laptop and quickly pulled up a search engine, typing in *Fernando Garcia de la Vega, bullfighter*. Links for the name "Garcia de la Vega" popped up. More than two thousand results. Wow. She selected "search images," and photos of the devastatingly handsome Fernando flooded the screen. Fernando as a boy beside his equally attractive father, both dressed in full matador regalia... Fernando in the ring at twenty-two... A more mature Fernando with a gorgeous woman on his arm at an animal rights fundraiser in Madrid... What?

Eve clicked on the related story and began reading. It seemed that Fernando's grandfather had not only been one of Spain's most prized matadors, he'd also introduced a new form of "*a mano*" bullfighting in which the bull was killed cleanly with one stroke. Picadors were still present in the ring but only for show. None were allowed to injure or torment the bull. This was a game of pure skill, man versus beast, each with his own pointed weapon. One matador's blade against two deadly horns. His insistence on fighting this way had made him more than a famous matador; he'd become something of a folk hero, known for his respect for the bulls as well as his utter bravery. He'd died in the ring before the age of fifty, just as his son—Fernando's father— had, leaving behind an enormous estate.

Eve returned to the images, studying the one of Fernando as a boy who appeared to be about eight. She scanned the date of the picture, mentally calculating that Fernando must now be in his early thirties. Jessica was twenty-eight, and beautiful and talented. She hadn't had the best luck with men to date, but that didn't mean she'd have to run off and marry some guy in Spain! If Eve had the leave-time and the money, she'd get on a plane herself and talk some sense into Jess. Eve drew a deep breath, hoping that wouldn't be necessary. Eve twisted her hair back up and penned it in place. Surely, Jess would come around on her own and quickly extract herself from that *marriage by mistake*. If she didn't, Eve might just have to go begging to her boss and break out the credit card. What else on earth were best friends for?

"Jessica! Wait up!" Fernando called, galloping after her.

It had been years since she'd been on a horse, and she delighted in the freedom of the ride.

Fernando gave a loud call, and his bay Andalusian stallion picked up speed, drawing alongside Jess's gray mare.

"You are moving awfully fast for a woman in your condition." He shot her a charming grin. "Not that I'd expect anything less from a spitfire like you."

Jess slowed her horse to a trot as Fernando kept pace. "The pregnancy thing was really over the top," she said, giving him a glance. "Even for a flamboyant inventor like you."

He tilted his chin in her direction, easily reining in his horse. "I know, and I apologize for surprising you. It's just—when the idea occurred, it fit so perfectly with everything else."

"What everything else?"

He gestured to a grove of olive trees up ahead in the distance. "We'll find some afternoon shade over there. Let's stop for a while and rest the horses."

Jess was irritated he kept putting her off. She was ready for the truth and deserved it now.

Fernando dismounted, then held out his hand. She accepted his help in getting off her horse, nearly sliding into his arms. He was ruggedly handsome out here on these windswept plains, the sun dancing above them in a nearly cloudless azure sky.

"Would you mind holding this?" he asked, depositing the satchel in her arms. He withdrew a light picnic blanket from its interior and spread it beneath the craggy branches of an ancient tree.

"Won't you sit?" he said, retrieving the bag to lay it on the ground, where he kneeled beside it.

Jess sat uncertainly at a safe distance, taking in the lovely landscape, the ranch, and the riding ring barely visible beyond the rolling vineyards. "How much property do you own?" she asked.

"Enough to get by," he said, uncorking the wine. "Although it's not really mine." He handed her a plastic cup filled to the brim with the lush, aromatic wine.

"It smells divine," she said, taking a sip and appreciating its full-bodied warmth and peppery finish. "Hmm. Is this one of yours?"

"A Bodega Garcia 2005. Do you like it?"

Jess more than liked it. It was fabulous, as was this place. Yet, she reminded herself, Fernando hadn't taken her into the country for some casual wine tasting. There were more serious matters at play. "It's delicious," she said, cupping her glass in both hands. "Now, your story?"

Fernando sighed, worry lines creasing his brow. "You're terribly angry with me, aren't you?"

"It takes two to tango, Fernando. I'm not saying all of this is your fault. I played a part in what happened yesterday too."

He turned toward her with a penetrating look. "That's what I don't understand. Why did you?"

Jess felt a lurch of emotion as he dissected her with his earnest green gaze. "I…don't know."

He leaned toward her with a husky whisper. "Oh, but I think you do."

He drew nearer, his mouth hovering over hers. Jess cursed herself for so badly wanting his kiss. His kisses had been so tantalizing last night, they'd made her lose all sense of reason. And it wasn't just the way he'd held her. When he'd looked deep in her eyes and said that one thing, she'd inexplicably believed him as she had no man before.

"Why did you?"

Fernando reached out and cupped her chin in his hand. "Because, *querida,* when I saw you standing there in that garden, with that beautiful smile on your lips, I knew with a certainty that I'd have to claim them. That I wouldn't rest until I made you mine."

"It was a simple sexual attraction."

"There was nothing simple about it," he said, brushing his lips to hers.

Jess closed her eyes as her heart stilled. She couldn't let herself do this, but she couldn't stop herself either. His masculine scent washed over her as she felt his palm press into the small of her back.

"Jessica," he said, resting his forehead on hers. "When I tell you the truth about this morning, I don't want you to believe that anything last night was a lie." And then to prove it, he kissed her deeply, with a skill and a passion that made her lose grip of her wine, sending the contents of her cup sloshing sideways.

"Your sister's riding pants," she said, nearly breathless.

"They'll wash," he said, tenderly stroking her thigh.

"Fernando," Jess gasped, pulling back. "We can't."

He studied her a thoughtful moment as she gazed at him wide-eyed.

"Then we won't," he said with a quick peck on her lips.

She shivered involuntarily in spite of herself. This man had a way of completely undoing her.

"We'll have a little something to eat first." He pulled several small bundles from his bag, along with a small knife and a cutting board.

"While we talk?"

"Of course," he said, handing her a napkin for her slacks. "Then afterwards, I'll let you decide."

"Decide what?"

Fernando shot her a sexy grin as he refilled her wine.

"Whether or not I'm the husband of your dreams."

Chapter Four

"So, it's not true," Jess said with relief. "We're not really married?"

Fernando took a slow sip of his wine, perusing her over the rim of his cup. "In the eyes of the church, we are."

"And in the eyes of the state?"

"That's more problematic," he bantered back.

"More problematic how?"

"Jessica," he said with a lingering look, "I told you the paperwork takes time to process."

"Seven to ten days," she replied, restating what he'd told her earlier.

"Best-case scenario."

"Because everything's been submitted to the magistrate in Seville?"

"La Esperanza del Corazón is a small town," he said deferentially. "Anything here has to be sent to a higher authority."

"Fernando," she said, meaning it absolutely. "I need you to level with me. What's in this pretense of a marriage for you?"

He set down his cup, then took her own and put it aside. "Everything is at stake for me. More than you imagine."

"Like?" she pressed.

Fernando heaved a sigh, surveying the panorama around him.

"Like..." he said, with a weighty frown, "this place here. The ranch. My mother's sustenance."

Jessica sat up a little straighter as north winds rippled, stirring the branches above them.

"I don't understand."

"My grandfather was a proud man. Proud and stubborn too. He decided long ago that he wished his legacy to continue. His commitment to the bulls, his attachment to this land…"

"And?"

"He wrote it all down," Fernando said. "He wasn't about to take chances. Ernesto Garcia de la Vega wanted to ensure that his legacy would continue."

"In what way?"

"In a way that ensured a continuation of the line."

"You're talking you, now?"

"I'm talking me and you. Don't you understand what this means? How huge this is?"

She shook her head, utterly confused by his confession.

"Jessica," he said, fiercely meeting her gaze. "If I don't find a bride and produce offspring by the time I'm thirty-two, this whole thing is for naught. This estate, my inheritance, any support meant to go to my mother…will all fall through."

"But how?" she asked, incredulous.

"It's in the codicils of my grandfather's will," he answered flatly. "Either I marry my match and we produce an heir by my thirty-second birthday, or the entire estate goes to the Catholic Church of La Esperanza del Corazón."

"No," she said, fascinated and compelled at once.

"Please, tell me that you'll help," he said, meeting her eyes. "My mother is a strong woman, it's true, possibly as fierce as they come. But this ranch is her home. She buried my father here and longs to have her final resting place beside him."

Jess thought of her own mother and each of the struggles she'd endured as a single mom. As harsh as

Señora Garcia de la Vega had come off during their lunch, Jess knew the woman was simply being protective of her only son. Jess frankly admired her for raising two children solo. She knew from her mother's experience that task wasn't easy. She didn't know about Fernando's sister, but the man himself had turned out decently enough. Perhaps better, in many ways, than she'd initially understood. While Fernando could be brash in business, there was a softer side to him she hadn't been privy to until late last night. When he'd held her in his arms, he'd done so with a tenderness and a passion that no woman in her right mind could ignore. Jess had found it impossible to resist his advances, when—in truth—she ached for him just as desperately as he wanted her. It wasn't just about sex; it was in the way he looked at her, in the way he promised that one thing she'd longed her entire lifetime to hear… And now there was another layer to him still, that of the caring and devoted son. Jess couldn't help but find his commitment to family instantly appealing. Still, this notion was absurd. He couldn't actually believe she'd consider it.

"There has to be another way," she said. "Couldn't you buy the ranch for your mother yourself? You make good money in Madrid."

"Not *that* good."

"How good is that?"

He studied at her sincerely. "This piece of land alone is worth over two billion dollars."

"Billion?"

Fernando solemnly shook his head. "That's a lot to spend on holy water."

"But our…marriage…was so incidental. Surely, you didn't plan on that."

"No, it was an utter, and delightful, surprise," he said with a warming smile. "In fact, it was the best birthday present I've ever had."

"Yesterday was your birthday?" she asked, intrigued.

"Early birthday present," he said, correcting himself. "My actual birthday's still eight days away. I'll be thirty-one."

Jess felt an instant flood of relief. "Well, then, you're still good for another year!"

He raised his brow at her. "Babies take nine months."

"Come on," she said. "Since you didn't bank on marrying me, you must have had a backup plan. What's wrong with that?"

Everything was wrong with that, as far as Fernando was concerned. He studied her a long while, her cheeks flushed in the early evening breeze. Though he'd always found her attractive, he'd never truly understood her beauty until now. Jessica was unlike anyone he'd ever known. She wasn't just some pretty face. She was as smart as she was strong, he was betting even as strong as his mother. To date, he'd not met any other woman of that caliber, and it both fascinated and terrified him.

The fact was, Fernando did have a backup plan—in the form of what most Americans called *the little black book.* He'd known for some time now that if the right woman didn't come along on her own, he'd have to start taking serious measures by the time he turned thirty-one. It caused a knot in the pit of his stomach to think he'd likely have to settle. That was why he'd put the idea off, more and more over time. While there were plenty of eligible women who might fit the bill, Fernando deplored the thought of marrying someone for sheer convenience. Though he still held a fondness for some of his old girlfriends, it was hard to imagine fanning those flames into full-blown passion.

Perhaps with effort and time, a deeper feeling might blossom over the years. But this was tough to believe when Fernando wasn't even sure what type of emotion he was capable of. Up until last night, he didn't think he had sentimentality in him. But when Jessica had turned those beautiful blue eyes toward his, he'd found a lump in his throat and a pounding in his chest that were completely unfamiliar. As tough as she was, she'd revealed a certain fragility when she'd bared her soul and shared her secret burden. He couldn't help but hold her close and swear to her he'd make everything right. And he'd meant it too. This morning's sun and his new sobriety hadn't weakened his commitment.

"Jessica, I'd be lying to say I wasn't feeling the squeeze of the timeline closing in. I understood I was under the gun with my birthday drawing near."

She gasped at the harsh realization. "You took advantage of me. I just happened to be in the right place at the right time."

"That's not so!" he said with a firmness that took her aback. She startled, notably shaken, making him feel an outrageous fool.

"Forgive me," he said, collecting himself. "It's just that what you said is so far from true."

"Far from true, Fernando? You just admitted to me yourself you were under pressure to find a bride."

"Maybe that's why I let myself go."

"I don't understand," she said kindly.

Fernando stroked his chin, carefully considering his next words. "You've seen how I am at work."

"Tough as nails."

"I'm tough when I need to be, yes. I'm also used to being in charge. So are you," he went on with a grin, "which leads to some interesting…conversations."

"Confrontations are more like it," she said with a lighthearted laugh.

He gave her a lingering look. "True," he said, "but neither of us has been mortally wounded yet.

"In any case," he continued, "the pressure was starting to build. It was like my whole life had been decided for me, and I had no say in the matter. My birthday was coming up, and I'd have to find someone—just anyone—to fit the bill. The last thing in the world I wanted to do was think about it. I wanted to be young and carefree like any other thirty-year-old man without such weighty family responsibilities. And then the business associates with whom you and I had intended to share dinner made plans that fell through. Suddenly, it was just the two of us."

"The two of us and a lot of sangria, as I recall," she said with a modest blush.

He reached across the blanket and took her hand. "I wouldn't take any of it back, Jessica. Nothing that happened yesterday evening. I don't know how to explain this to you, but at the moment, marrying you not only seemed the right thing to do, it was like the fates had left me no choice. First, there you were—with those incredible eyes and that angelic smile—and then there was Padre Domingo. It was like nothing in my life had made sense up until that point, and then suddenly everything did. Can you understand what I'm telling you?"

Jess felt the warmth in her cheeks. "That you believe this was meant to happen?"

He nodded, then took her hand and gave the back of it a light kiss.

"Yes, *querida*. I do."

Jess cursed her inner voice for saying she believed it too. This was the most outlandish situation she'd ever found herself in. And yet why did her heart beat faster each time his eyes lingered on hers? Why did part of her so want to believe he'd been put in her path for a reason? A reason that would bring her a better life of comfort and companionship. And, quite possibly, the one thing that up until now she'd refused to believe in? But, she couldn't let herself believe it. Not here, not now, not with this handsome matador, for crying out loud. She was in Spain. *Spain!* Over three thousand miles from home. Jess had a commitment to family too, and hers lay across the Atlantic. As did her job, and very best friend on earth. She had to pull herself out of this fantasy while she still had the strength to walk away.

"I know you mean well," she said softly. "And all that you've shared, your motivation for helping your mother, for saving your family's ranch. Those are all things I understand; really I do. And I admire you, Fernando. Admire you greatly for putting your mother's happiness above your own and wanting to do right by her and your grandfather's bequest. But I'm not the right girl for this job. Surely, you'll have lots of other takers."

Fernando hung his head and turned away. "Yes," he said quietly. "Yes, I'm sure you're right. Dozens, maybe hundreds."

She reached out and lightly touched his arm. He pulled away.

"The sun is sinking low," he said. "I think it's time we pack up and head in. I told my mother we'd be back by nightfall."

"I'm sorry," Jess said past the tenderness in her throat.

He leveled her with a gaze devoid of emotion. "Don't be," he said. "I'm not. Not sorry for anything."

He helped her up on her horse, then mounted his own. Fernando righted himself in his saddle.

"The first thing on Tuesday," he said without looking at her, "I'll take you to Seville. Just as you wish, we'll get this annulled."

Chapter Five

Ana María Garcia de la Vega pulled a tiny garment from the mahogany hope chest at the foot of her bed. The pure linen christening gown had been hand-embroidered by her grandmother and worn for generations. She gently strummed her fingertips across the daintily stitched white flowers adorning the piece's bodice. When her daughter Margarita had worn it, Ana María hadn't known she'd have no future children to dress in this little frock. She and her husband, Ernesto, had planned a large family. *"Six children at least,"* he'd said, the setting sun warming his eyes. He'd taken her in his arms and kissed her in a way that had melted her heart and weakened her knees. While her mother had warned her of the *responsibilities* of a honeymoon, she'd never imagined she'd enjoy taking to the task so much.

When Ernesto died at forty-nine, Ana María had been just thirty-three. Fernando was eight and Margarita barely four. There was time for one or two more, at least. But time ran out on them far earlier than either of them intended. Ana María cast a sad gaze to the window, watching as dusk settled over the hacienda. She heard horses approaching from afar and knew it was Fernando and Jessica returning from their ride. Even if Jessica was experienced with horses, Fernando should have known better than to take the chance. Ana María held the small gown to her chest, realizing she'd never actually considered how it might feel to be a grandmother. Jessica certainly was beautiful, and, if she worked in Fernando's business, obviously smart. But what of her family? Her background?

The Garcia de la Vegas could trace their ancestry back seven generations—on both sides. Americans weren't like that. Most of them were divorced and had no concept of family beyond the immediate. Even many of the closest relatives remained estranged, according to what Ana María had gathered from her perusal of the papers and study of American media. But if Fernando loved her… Ana María felt a lump in her throat. Who was she to deny true love, if this was real? Her parents hadn't exactly been pleased she'd selected a matador as a groom. And yet they'd eventually come around, blessing them both with a lavish wedding and the gift of this ranch. Ana María had been raised here with her two brothers, neither of whom had survived to adulthood. Life was cruel that way, taking away the people you loved.

Ana María wiped her brow with the back of her arm, scolding herself for becoming sentimental. Sentimentality was a weakness reserved for those able to afford it. She carefully folded the baptismal gown, tucking it back in its nest. Though she'd never weighed it concretely, she knew Fernando would make a marvelous father. There was a man who understood the value of family and stuck by them. He'd been so good to her and to his sister Margarita. Ana María couldn't imagine him lavishing anything but undying affection on the woman he'd picked as his bride, and any offspring they produced.

Ana María heard the heavy door swing shut downstairs and felt an instant wave of shame. Though she'd been cordial enough at lunch, she hadn't precisely proved the welcoming mother-in-law. After all he'd done for her, who was she to doubt Fernando's judgment? But…an American from Brooklyn! *Ay.* Ana María sighed heavily and closed the hope chest, securing it shut with its sculpted key. At least Fernando was moving forward, she supposed.

Margarita, in her fancy flat in Barcelona, didn't even have a boyfriend.

Fernando entered the foyer and dropped his satchel with a petulant scowl, Jessica trailing in his wake.

"Did you have a nice time?" Ana María asked as he breezed past her and headed for the study. Moments later, she heard the clattering of Waterford crystal and knew he was pouring himself a scotch from the family decanter. She and Jessica startled as the study door snapped shut.

"I think I'm going to lie down," Jessica said, appearing a bit disheveled. Her hair was tousled from the wind, her complexion lightly flushed. Her blue eyes were cloudy and troubled.

"Are you all right?" Ana María inquired.

Jessica blinked, then stared at her, her color deepening. "It was just a bit of a ride."

"I knew Fernando shouldn't have—"

"No, please," Jessica interrupted. "It's okay. It's not that I'm sick or anything. Just tired."

Ana María studied her sympathetically. "Of course you are, dear."

Jessica headed for the stairs with a zombie-like gaze, then began her slow ascent.

"Can I bring you some tea?" Ana María asked. "Decaffeinated?"

"Thanks, but no," she said in a warbling voice.

Now, Ana María had heard of lovers' spats. But it seemed a bit early in this brand-new marriage for them to be developing problems already.

She considered talking to Fernando but then thought better of it. Best to leave him alone and give him time to sort things out. Whatever the cause, it was sure to be something minor. The lovebirds would settle things by bedtime, if not before.

Ana María's gaze followed Jessica up the stairs, a gentle melancholy taking hold. *Ah, to be young and in love, like these two.* Ernesto may have been gone awhile, but it wasn't so long that Ana María had forgotten.

Dinner was a somber affair. Ana María sat at the elegantly set table, staring at the two empty chairs beside her. Though their places had been set, neither Fernando nor Jessica had appeared for the meal. Fernando had claimed he wasn't hungry, and Jessica—feeling woozy—had petitioned to have a tray sent up to her room. Whatever had transpired during their ride had clearly driven a wedge between them. Then again, misunderstandings often happened early in a marriage. Fernando and Jessica were just now getting to know each other as husband and wife. This put them in a different place than lovers. Once you'd bound yourselves to one another for eternity, you started to view certain things differently.

Ana María knew the young couple had many details to work out, particularly with Jessica coming from the United States. A sudden panic seized her. Surely, they weren't considering moving to America? What a disaster that would be. Fernando in New York, a vast ocean in between them. And what of the grandchild? Clearly, it would be best for him or her to be raised here, on this beautiful hacienda with its stable of horses and the freedom to roam the land. Of course, Jessica's family would be disappointed with her moving so far away. But it seemed she'd already made that choice, didn't it? Nobody married a Garcia de la Vega without knowing what that meant. There was a weight of responsibility, not just in maintaining the family name but also in continuing its vein of philanthropy that had proved a boon to the poorest regions of this country.

Ana María took a sip of wine, considering what she might do to help. For one thing, she could make Fernando's new bride feel more welcome here. For another, she could ensure that Jessica became so taken with La Esperanza del Corazón that she would never want to leave.

There was a sharp knock at the door, followed by Fernando's husky request. "Jessica. A moment, please."

Jess set down her fork, realizing her efforts at eating were failing anyway. While the roast pork and potatoes in a sherry glaze was delicious, she'd scarcely been able to swallow two bites. Ever since the end of their ride and Fernando's pronouncement that he'd set her free, she'd been inexplicably depressed. The fact that he'd refused to meet her eyes afterward had only deepened that effect.

While he hadn't said it so many words, it was clear that Jessica had wounded him. Could he have really meant what he'd said? That he'd developed actual feelings for her?

Jessica slid her tray back on the dresser top and quickly adjusted her hair in the mirror.

"Come in!" she said, angling toward the door.

He stepped into the room, appearing more handsome than ever, despite his brooding expression. "I've only come to get my things," he said.

He was still angry with her. "Fernando," she said softly. "You do know we're doing the right thing?"

"Which thing is that?" he asked with a flat stare.

Jess felt her breath constrict as she doubted the sincerity of her own words. "Going to Seville."

He studied her with a mix of melancholy and annoyance.

"I already told you I would not keep you here."

Jess's words raced from her heart to her mouth, bypassing her brain. She felt consumed by emotion, abandoned yet again. In the light of the moon, she'd shared her dark history. No one who'd professed to love her had ever stuck around. How could she have imagined that Fernando was different? "But you promised…" she began, pain etched in her voice.

"I know what I promised," he said, pursing his lips. "I said that I would never leave you. And I meant it." He paused for emphasis as Jess's heart thumped against her chest. "But, it seems to me that things have turned quite the other way around. You're the one running away."

Jess's face flashed hot as her tongue went numb. Of course he was right, so what could she say?

Fernando crossed to the armoire and withdrew a large feather pillow and a few blankets.

There was a tug in her heart telling her she shouldn't let him go. That she should insist he stay here so they could talk things out. But to what end? So that she might fall back into his sturdy arms and get swept into his bed?

"I'll sleep in the study," he said, turning away. "Breakfast is at eight."

Chapter Six

Eve stretched an arm out from under the covers and nabbed her cell phone off the nightstand. Who could be calling at this ungodly hour?

"Hello?" she said groggily into the mouthpiece.

"Evie, it's me. Jess."

Eve pushed herself upright into a sitting position in her yellow polka-dot pajamas. "Jess, what's wrong?"

"Nothing's wrong. It's all good. I'm going to fix it."

"The marriage?"

"I talked to Fernando, and it's all arranged. He'll take me to Seville tomorrow to get things annulled."

"What day is it now?" Eve asked with a yawn.

"Monday."

Eve sleepily studied the numbers on the nearby clock.

"Good God, Jess. It's two a.m. here."

"I know, and I'm sorry. I just..." Her voice fell off in a whisper.

"Jess?"

There was no answer at first, and for a moment, Eve feared she'd lost the connection.

"Jess, are you still there?"

"I'm here." She sounded fragile and exhausted.

"You don't sound so hot."

"I didn't sleep well."

"He kept you up all night—again?"

"Yes, but not like that. I had the worst insomnia, Evie. The *worst*. As crazy as it seems, I'm feeling all torn up about this, like maybe I'm not doing the right thing."

Eve blinked hard, switching on the light. "You are talking crazy. Of course what you're doing is right! You made a whopper of a mistake, and you're lucky it's not too late to have it undone."

There was a pregnant pause on the line that sent shivers racing down Eve's spine.

"Jess," Eve said, her breathing measured. "Tell me you are not changing your mind?"

"No, of course not!" she shot back a little too quickly. "Why on earth would you think that?"

Eve massaged her forehead, worried for her best friend. Jess hadn't just married a matador; she'd apparently lost all sense of reason.

"What the name of that town where you are again?"

"La Esperanza del Corazón. Why?"

Because if Jess didn't come to her senses soon, Eve might just have to pull out her platinum credit card and fly there. "Call me on Tuesday after everything's taken care of."

"All right," Jess responded weakly.

"Jess!" Eve said sternly. "You *are* going through with it?"

Jess opened the door to find Consuelo smiling and holding a tray arranged with fresh flowers and coffee. "A morning treat from Doña Ana María," she said. "A little something to get you started."

"I thought breakfast was downstairs?" Jess asked with surprise.

"Oh yes, it is," Consuelo said, merrily breezing past her to set the tray on the dresser. "This is just for while you're getting ready."

Jess cinched the large cotton robe more tightly around her waist. It had been supplied by Fernando on their wedding night and was luxurious in its comfort.

She surveyed the silver coffee service and accompanying basket brimming with homemade pastries, thinking there was enough here to feed a family.

"You're eating for two," Consuelo quipped as if reading her mind. "And don't worry" she said heading for the door. The coffee is decaffeinated."

Jess poured herself a cup of coffee with steamed milk and carried it to the seat by the window, its heavenly aroma wafting upwards. The morning sun spread its warmth across the landscape surrounding Casa de la Vega, encompassing its stark beauty. Jess felt as if she'd been transported into a dream or catapulted somehow back in time, to a place where life was simpler. There couldn't be any greater contrast to her busy life in New York than the serenity of La Esperanza del Corazón.

She couldn't help but wonder how things might have played out if she and Fernando had had an actual courtship. The chemistry between them as business colleagues had been brewing beneath the surface for months. What might have happened if they'd acted upon it sooner? Had even started dating and developed a transatlantic relationship? There might have been ups and downs, but ultimately, one of two things would have occurred. Either things would have ended between them, which would have been the most likely outcome, given Jess's track record. Or, there was an outside chance they might have fallen in love and decided—thoughtfully and intelligently—to make the bond between them permanent.

Given more time to get to know him and consider the prospect of their life together, what choice would Jess have made? There were so many things to take into account, like their separate commitments to their jobs and where they might eventually live as a couple. And then there was the prospect of children to consider.

Jess brought a palm to her belly; her face flushed at the thought of carrying Fernando's child. While she felt awful about deceiving his mother, she had to admit that the notion of making a baby with Fernando wasn't completely abhorrent. In fact, she probably wouldn't have gone so far as to imagine it had he not invented that little story about her being in a maternal way. In any case, she hoped Fernando would tell his mother the truth soon. Everyone here was starting to treat Jess with deference due to her pregnancy, and that simply wasn't fair. It was bad enough to be thought of as married, but expecting a baby added a whole new layer to this blanket of deception. Perhaps Fernando was waiting until all was resolved in Seville before coming clean with his mother. Or perhaps, Jess thought with a hopeful start, he'd talked to her already!

Jess recalled Consuelo's morning words, realizing that was unlikely. And that was terrible too. The longer this ruse went on with Fernando's family, the harder it would be to reveal the truth. And the more awful she'd feel about herself, for having let Fernando get away with it. Something had to be done, and soon.

Fernando approached his mother as she tended the roses in her garden. "Mamá," he began tentatively. "I have something to discuss with you."

Ana María adjusted the brim of her wide straw hat. "And I with you, my son." She carefully set down her pruning shears and cleaned her hands on her apron. "I'm afraid I haven't been quite fair to you and your new wife."

"Precisely what we need to talk about."

"Yes," she answered, a sincere apology in her eyes. "It's true. I know I've failed you."

"Failed me?" Fernando said, taken aback. If anyone was the let-down party in this twosome, it was him, and he knew it. "I don't see how—"

"Yesterday at lunch, I was less than hospitable," she said, cutting him off. "It's just that it all came as such a surprise."

"I know. I understand."

"I let the shock get the better of me. I really shouldn't have, but I did."

Fernando laid his hands on her shoulders. "Mamá, listen to me. About Jessica…"

His mother's face brightened. "Well, there she is now! And looking even lovelier than before. The rest must have served her well."

Fernando turned toward the house to see Jessica standing on the patio, uncertainly glancing around. The breakfast table was set, yet empty.

"Oh dear, is it eight already?" Ana María asked. "Please, make my apologies to Jessica. I'll dash on in the house and clean up. Be back in a flash."

Fernando sighed with dismay as his mother scurried off toward the garden shed to deposit her tools. He really needed to tell her the truth, but sharing such dismal news over breakfast hardly seemed civilized. He shoved his hands in his pockets and trudged toward the house, considering how he might put things. There really wasn't an easy way around it. He'd just have to come straight out and tell her the whole thing was a lie. But it hadn't been, starting out. That was the hard part. Jessica caught sight of him and waved, her flowing sundress rippling in the morning breeze. She was a sight to behold by the trellis, her golden hair catching sparkles of sunlight. Fernando felt a pang of regret, knowing he'd have to let her go. That seemed such a contrary thing to do, when every ounce of his being argued that she belonged right here.

He sent her a soft, sad smile, then made his way along the path, snapping a beautiful red rose off its stem along the way. His mother wouldn't appreciate his pilfering her garden, but he could no more stop himself from securing this impromptu offering than he'd been able to quell his desire for Jessica last night. He'd barely slept a wink in the study, tossing and turning… Wanting nothing more than to sneak up into that bed and kiss her languorously. Perhaps if he made love to her long—and perfectly—enough, she'd ultimately change her mind? Fernando chided himself for letting such absurd, romantic notions fill his head. The sooner he faced reality, the better. Jessica Bloom wanted nothing more than to be rid of him. And, soon enough, her wish would be his command.

Fernando stepped onto the patio, extending a pretty red rose in Jessica's direction. She felt the warmth in her cheeks as he captured her in his hypnotic green gaze.

"Forgive me for being forward, but it reminded me of you."

"I hardly think it's forward, considering that we're married," she said, deflecting the moment.

"You don't have to remind me."

She accepted the flower and brought it lightly to her nose, inhaling its sweet scent. "Thank you," she said, meeting his eyes. "It's beautiful."

"Well, this is what I like to see!" Ana María said cheerily, stepping over the great room's threshold. "Two lovebirds in the morning, making up."

Jess and Fernando exchanged glances as Ana María took her seat.

"Oh sorry, Mamá." He scuttled over to help her with her chair and then assisted Jess with hers.

Within seconds, Consuelo appeared to pour fresh-squeezed juice and serve up a bounty of aromatic foods.

"So, what are your plans for the morning?" Ana María asked, spreading her napkin on her lap.

Jessica stared at Fernando and blinked.

"We...haven't really had time to talk about it," he said.

"Wonderful, then I have a suggestion."

Jess turned her attention on the older woman. "Oh?"

"Fernando," she encouraged with a smile. "Why don't you take Jessica into town today? Show her around, let her get acquainted with our nice little village."

"I think that sounds like a fine idea," Jess piped in. And it did too. Anything sounded better than sitting around here, second-guessing her decision all day through.

"You do?" Fernando asked with mild surprise.

"Absolutely." She took a heavenly bite of huevos rancheros cooked with chorizo, and to perfection. "How soon can we get started?"

Fernando met her gaze with a puzzled frown. "Just as soon as you'd like."

"Fernando!" his mother scolded, slapping his arm with a whack. "Where are your manners? Show some enthusiasm!"

Fernando glanced at his mother and then slowly turned his gaze on Jess. "I apologize," he said with devilishly disarming eyes, "if I came off as *anything* less than enthusiastic. As you're aware, I'm quite capable of giving you my focused attention."

Jess gave a little laugh and fanned her face with her napkin. She be damned if he didn't look like he wanted to take her, right then and there—on top of this linen tablecloth! Jess felt a rash of heat sweep from her temples to her toes, but the hottest spots were those situated somewhere in between.

"Perhaps you two should take a little nap before heading out?" Ana María noted astutely.

"Excellent idea, Mother," he said, not pulling his gaze from Jessica's while he lightly kissed the back of her hand.

Jess's pulse whipped into overdrive as Fernando's lips lingered an extra-long moment.

"You're looking a little tired, my love," he said in a husky whisper. "Why don't we finish up? Then I'll take you to lie down."

Fernando firmly took Jess's hand and led her up the stairs. Okay, she had twenty-two steps to think about it. The trouble was, she'd already lost count of which one they were on, and they were nearly to the landing. Hopping back into bed with her new husband wasn't exactly the best way to start an annulment. And they *were* getting this annulled or stopped from processing, whichever one applied. Whatever had to happen once they got to Seville. But there were still a lot of hours between now and tomorrow.

Fernando reached the upstairs hall and pulled her up and off the last step and into his arms. "You know," he said in a sexy whisper, "my mother never would have condoned this if she'd known all the paperwork hadn't gone through."

"You said we were married in the eyes of the church."

His mouth hovered over hers as he backed her up against the wall. "It feels real enough to me."

Fire raged through her as he captured her mouth with his and kissed her deeply, his touch tracing the line of her throat, then trailing to her cleavage. Jess gasped involuntarily, her knees threatening to give way. That was some silly cliché from the movies. A woman didn't *actually* swoon in a man's arms. Then again, most men weren't built like Fernando. She'd certainly never met anyone of his...aptitude, the most pressing part of which pushed rock-hard against her thigh.

He brought his mouth to the side of her neck, then nibbled slightly as he squeezed one breast and then the other. "So good," he breathed. "I want to taste more."

Jess felt her panties moisten and knew she was doomed. All she wanted to do now was step out of them. Fernando's hand slid up her thigh and under her dress, making her want to rip it off completely.

"Fernando," she moaned, grappling with the words, "we're still in the hall."

He pulled back in a heated flush, a savage passion in his eyes. "I can fix that." Then, in one deft movement, he unlatched the door and kicked it open. The next thing Jess knew, she was airborne, swept into his arms and cradled to his sturdy chest. He spoke as he carried her over the threshold, his voice husky with desire. "If you don't mind," he said with a sultry gaze, "I'd like to make love to my new wife...for as long as she can stand."

That might be quite a while, Jess reasoned. But she didn't have to say so. He'd already laid her on the bed and was stripping away her panties. Jess knew she might regret this later, but it certainly seemed the right thing to do now. She gasped as he entered her, feeling as though she'd found the place in the world where she'd always belonged.

"I do love you, Jessica," he whispered between kisses. "I'm praying that someday soon you'll believe it."

She believed it now, oh yes, she did, and she wanted this feeling to go on forever. Jess wrapped her arms around his neck and kissed him back, hoping this wasn't an illusion. Even if it was, she didn't care to stop it. She'd never experienced anyone like Fernando in her life, and this morning he was all hers.

"Are you newlyweds going to want dinner?" It was Ana María's voice outside the door.

Jess opened her eyes to find herself wrapped in Fernando's arms, the sheets twisted around them.

"We'll be down in a minute, Mamá!" Fernando called, snuggling Jess closer. "You *are* hungry?" he asked Jess in a whisper.

"Starved," she answered truthfully.

"Good," he said with a firm kiss on her lips. "That means I did my husbandly duty."

He'd more than done his husbandly duty. Given the various kinds of attention he'd administered, Jess feared it would be weeks before she'd ever walk again.

"I'll say," she said, smiling. "I'm honestly not sure how well my knees will hold up after that."

He shot her a sexy grin. "I can carry you, if you'd like."

"Your carrying me is what landed us in bed."

"So it did," he replied, lightly caressing her cheek as he kissed her again.

"What time do you think it is?" she asked.

"It must be around two o'clock."

"In the afternoon? We've been here half the day?"

"I wouldn't say it was a waste, would you?"

"No, it was…marvelous."

"Marvelous?" he asked, with an amused grin. "That makes me feel pretty special."

"You are special," she said, meaning it absolutely. In an utterly confounding way, he was the most marvelous man she'd ever met.

Fernando's heart lit up at the sound. Was that hope springing from his new bride's lips? Was she actually starting to fall for him?

"You're not sorry, then?" he asked, holding her gaze.

Her beautiful blue eyes softened. "I'm not sorry that I met you, no. Not sorry that things became intimate between us…"

"And the wedding?"

She stiffened beneath the blankets. "Don't push it, Fernando."

"I'm sorry. I didn't mean to."

Jess sat up, covering herself with the duvet. "Don't you think we should get dressed? Your mother's waiting."

Fernando pressed his palms together and sighed. From one moment to the next, he couldn't tell if he stood a chance with this woman. Maybe he'd been a fool to believe one concentrated morning of loving would change her mind. "Fine. We'll go down and eat. Do you still want to head into town later?"

"Yes, I think we should. Don't you?"

"I actually wouldn't have minded if you'd suggested another nap."

She picked up a pillow and swatted him playfully.

"Ow! Watch where you aim that!"

"Protecting something?" she asked with a wicked grin.

Fernando might not totally understand her, but he knew her well enough to sense when she wanted more. "Yes, let me show it to you."

"Oh God, are you serious?"

He rolled her onto her back, clambering on top of her. "I think there are too many blankets between us."

She threw them back with reckless abandon and grabbed his naked rear.

"As long as we're still married…" she said, tilting up her chin.

"If ever I've seen a conflicted woman, it's you," he said, parting her knees.

"Maybe I need further convincing."

"Hmm," he said with a smile. "Is that what you Americans call this?"

Then he lowered his head as Jess gripped the covers and begged him over and over again not to stop.

Chapter Seven

Two hours later, and after a slightly embarrassing dinner during which Ana María sent repeated *knowing*—yet approving—looks at the newlyweds, Jess and Fernando were traveling up steep roads leading to the center of town. "This is breathtaking," Jess said, absorbing the beauty of the tiny whitewashed village as they climbed heavenward. Fernando had told her that La Esperanza del Corazón was known as one of *Los Pueblos Blancos* in this southern region of Spain. Two things in particular made this place special: an old monastery and an ancient castle, both of which perched on the highest points in these hills.

"I know it seemed different on Friday night. When we came to the church here, it was under the cloak of darkness."

"I seem to recall an awfully full moon," she said, warmth caressing her cheeks.

"Yes," he said, taking her hand. She let him hold it, sensing a new comfort between them. While Fernando owned the sort of sports car meant to be driven at great speeds, she was glad he took his time navigating the hairpin turns of this precipitous trek.

Big billowy clouds hovered above them, dotting a brilliant blue sky, as a small river snaked through the valley below.

"I see Casa de la Vega!" Jess proclaimed, pointing at the roving vineyards beyond a river bend. "It's fantastic. I had no idea of its scope until I saw it from up here."

"My grandfather bought quite a bit of land," Fernando answered. "His dream was to start a vineyard. He made that dream a reality."

"Your mother runs it now?"

"All on her own. I'm very proud of her."

"Fernando," she asked suddenly. "What do you plan to do in your retirement?"

"Well…" he said, drawing out the word. "According to the grand Garcia de la Vega family plan, I was to step down from running the business in Madrid and return to run things here."

"That's why you were selling out to International Global Telecom."

"Exactly."

"But you also had to find a wife."

"Too true."

"So, if it hadn't been me, it would have been someone else," she said, growing indignant.

"If it isn't you, then it sadly will be someone else." He glanced at her, a wry smile upon his lips. "But trust me when I say you are my absolute first choice."

Jessica thought about that all the way to the monastery. She didn't really care who Fernando married, did she? If it wasn't going to be her, it naturally would be someone else. Even if it weren't for the inheritance, a man as attractive as Fernando was bound to get snapped up. Likely sooner than later, if he started flashing around that below-the-belt matador scar.

When they arrived at the low brown building with a large wrought-iron gate, Fernando sprang from the car to circumvent it and open her door for her. Very few guys did this in New York. Then again, traditions were more antiquated in Spain. Outdated. That's right, Jess told herself, keep recalling the modern world you come from. A life over here could only feel out of place.

"When we're done touring the monastery and its tapestries, I'll take you to its *damasquinado* shop."

"What's that?" Jess asked.

"It's an incredible style of jewelry inlaid with gold and unique to Spain."

"Real gold?" Jess asked, stuck on that first part.

Fernando nodded. "The brothers were trained by the finest artisans in Toledo. They sell their wares here to help keep this monastery afloat."

Jess loved creeping through the monastery as Fernando led her by the hand. Everything here seemed so darkly lit and holy. She almost swore she heard chanting as they made their way through the circuitous halls, studying one Catholic relic after the next, but Fernando said she was imagining it.

Finally, they came to the shopping part, which excited her a little even though she didn't plan to buy anything. The tiny gift shop was nestled in a corner on the far side of a brightly lit courtyard, sporting fountains and flocked with birds the good friars kept fed.

"Don Fernando? Is that you?"

Fernando turned toward a shopkeeper who greeted him with a cheery smile on his plump, round face. "Brother Emilio! How good to see you!"

The men embraced fondly; then Fernando made his introductions. "I'm very pleased to have you meet my new bride."

Brother Emilio beamed. "Bride, did you say? Why, what wonderful news. I couldn't be more happy for the two of you."

Jess said her polite hellos while Brother Emilio gripped her firmly by the shoulders and gave each cheek a happy kiss.

"Brother Emilio was one of my earliest tutors," Fernando told Jess. "He taught me everything I know about numbers."

"Lessons that served you well," Brother Emilio said proudly.

"When I was bad," Fernando confessed confidentially, "my mother used to threaten to send me to the monastery to live with Brother Emilio if I didn't behave."

Jess laughed out loud. Fernando in a monastery. Hoo. "That would have been a waste," she said, the words slipping out before she could stop them. Jess felt her face flash hot, imagining she'd committed the most egregious faux pas. Poor Brother Emilio. Would he think she was insulting his chosen path of celibacy? Luckily, the good man took things in stride.

"I can certainly imagine that," Brother Emilio said with a jovial smile. "Now come, you two. Look around and pick out something you like. Anything at all. Consider it a wedding gift on behalf of the brothers here."

"Oh my, that's so nice of you," Jess said. "But we can't."

"I insist," Brother Emilio said.

"He insists," Fernando echoed with a tilt of his head.

"Why, thank you," Jess said, feeling herself blush. It hardly seemed right to tell Brother Emilio they weren't really married—or might not be for long—when the fact of the matter was they *were* quite hitched in the eyes of the church. For now, at least.

"Darling," Fernando said sweetly. "Why don't you select a little memento for the two of us while I catch up a bit with my old friend?"

"Are you sure?" Jess asked, feeling like a kid in a candy shop with a fist full of change.

"Absolutely. Just get something that reminds you of us."

There was a lot of stuff to admire, but most of it was jewelry. Very expensive jewelry, Jess thought, putting back a spectacular set of dangly *damasquinado* earrings that played beautifully against her hair.

One of the other brothers came over to assist her. "You like these, miss?" he asked, retrieving them back off the rack. "Very beautiful, yes?"

"Oh yes, totally marvelous." Fernando turned his head in her direction as she waved the shopkeeper off. "But not so much my style, thank you. I'm looking for something more simple, really." And she was too. She and Fernando couldn't rob the good brothers of such an extravagant piece. Besides, women's ear-wear didn't precisely sound like a couple's gift.

"I'll just browse a bit more," she said, stepping over to the book section to survey the leather bookmarks. There were signs in several languages stating the good brothers had made these by hand too. She picked one up, appreciating its heady leather scent and surveying its beautiful custom design. "Is this an olive branch?" she asked the helpful brother, still loitering close by.

"In the mouth of a dove," he answered. "It's a symbol of God's eternal love, and peace."

"And hopefulness?" Jess inquired, thinking she'd heard that somewhere.

"In La Esperanza del Corazón, one always finds hope," the brother said with a warming smile.

"A bookmark? That's all?" Brother Emilio asked, slipping the object into a bag.

"I think it's very fine, don't you?" she asked Fernando.

"I find it...fitting, in many ways," he agreed.

"Well, good. Just as long it makes you happy." Brother Emilio pursed his lips for a pronounced beat. "Are you sure you won't take two? One bookmark is awfully hard to share."

"But a husband and wife should share everything, don't you agree?" Fernando said, taking Jess's hand. "Perhaps we'll place it in the books we read to each other, like poetry."

"Or the Bible!" Jess interposed, believing that sounded right. No harm in earning a few extra points. She hadn't set foot in a church in a decade, but she was sure to have made up for a couple of years at least—just in one afternoon.

"What a lovely, romantic couple you make," Brother Emilio said with a jolly grin. "Here, señora," he said, handing Jess the bag. "Live long and enjoy."

"Jessica," Fernando said as they paused outside. "Would you mind waiting here while I stop in the men's room?"

"Oh no, that's fine," she said, thinking she'd better go as well. "I'll stop in the ladies too, then meet you back here.

Fernando stepped around the corner; then, when he was certain she'd gone, he slipped back into the gift shop to ask Brother Tomás to point out the piece of jewelry Jessica had found so marvelous.

"Fernando," Jess said when he parked his car in the main plaza abutting the towering structure. "You can't just walk up to the door of a castle, knock and say 'hello, may we come in?'"

"No?" he asked, playing his best poker face.

"Well, you said yourself the place is private. Owned by some family."

"Yes," he answered evenly. "Mine."

Jessica gulped back her surprise. "You mean...?"

"My great aunt's, really. My grandfather took pity on her status as a young widow, so he built her this *marvelous* place here."

Jessica suspiciously narrowed her eyes at his emphasis on the word.

"She's expecting us, I think," he said, leading her up the broad stone steps. Fernando delighted in Jessica's gaze, filled with wonderment and expectation. She'd probably never been in a real castle before, at least not one that was personally owned.

He pulled back the enormous bronze knocker boasting an openmouthed lion head and pounded it three times against the twelve-foot door. After a few moments, the large plank creaked open.

"Don Fernando," a rail-thin woman said, kissing him on both cheeks and pinching one extra hard.

"This is Antonia," he told Jess with a sideways glance. "She always likes to hurt me."

"Ha ha!" the old woman said, soundly swatting his arm. Fernando winced. "This *caballero* is such a joker!"

"Is she your aunt?" Jessica whispered to him.

"Oh no," he whispered back. "Antonia enjoys her jazzercise. Tía Margarita does not."

As if on cue, an ancient woman toddled forth on sturdy ankles, followed by a yapping dog.

"Ah, the happy couple has arrived!" she cried, sweeping Fernando and Jess into her arms and pressing each one to an ample breast. She smelled of sweat and rosemary perfume, a bit heavier on the rosemary side each passing year, Fernando noted.

"Tía Margarita, Antonia," Fernando said, deftly extracting himself from his tía's embrace. "May I introduce you to my new wife, Jessica..." Who was still, he saw, plastered to Tía Margarita's chest, a hint of desperation in her eyes. Fernando pried her loose, tucking her under a protective arm. "Isn't she lovely?"

Tía Margarita lifted the glasses on the chain around her neck to her eyes in order to survey her nephew's prize. "Oh *sí*," she said enthusiastically. "Quite!"

Jessica withdrew a tissue from her purse to dab her neck and brow as Tía Margarita's mutt darted furiously at her feet, baring its teeth between barks.

"Does he bite?" she asked, attempting to sound nonchalant.

"Never more than a little," Tía Margarita said. "And there's so little of you to take, Rudolfo couldn't take much, eh?"

"Why don't we all go inside?" Fernando suggested, seeing the townspeople in the plaza were starting to stare.

"Of course," Tía Margarita said with a smile, linking her arm through his.

As Antonia flanked Jessica on the other side, he could have sworn he heard her asking if Jessica was familiar with the Stairmaster.

Jess couldn't guess how high the ceilings were. They were vaulted and tall, like the inside of a cathedral, enormous chandeliers dripping throughout the halls. There were oversized, arched windows too, interspersed by large oil paintings and various works of art. It was more like being in a museum than a mansion. Not that she'd ever been in a mansion before. But galleries, she knew. Though those clearly housed less furniture. Everything was larger than life, huge carved pieces with mirrors surprising her around every turn. It certainly smelled musty and was dank as well. She was glad Fernando still had his arm around her, because the dankness seeped into her bones even at the height of summer.

"Having fun, *querida*?" he whispered into her ear, and she shivered, not from the cold but from the heat of his breath.

The truth was, she was having more than fun. Jess felt like she'd slipped down the rabbit hole into some imaginary realm and was enjoying the time of her life. Wait until she told Evie! Jess felt a rush of guilt, thinking of her best friend. She didn't know why, so she pushed the notion aside, attempting to live in the moment. She'd already committed herself to this day with Fernando, anyway, hadn't she?

"This is so cool," she said, eyes widening as they stepped into an expansive area opening onto a walled veranda.

"Maybe we should ask if you can borrow a sweater?" he said, feigning misunderstanding. "Or maybe," he said in a low rumble meant just for her, "I can warm you up later."

"Are you all right, Jessica?" Tía Margarita asked, turning from where she'd just plunked her puppy on the table. An elaborate spread was laid for tea, three high-backed chairs facing the pastoral view. Jess watch in awe as Tía Margarita poured and little Rudolfo eagerly thrust his nose into a cup. "You appear a little flushed."

"She was just saying that she's cold."

"Fernando!" Jess scolded under her breath.

Tía Margarita wrinkled up her pudgy brow. "Oh dear, that certainly won't do. Antonia," she said, instructing her maid, who was setting the last plate of biscuits on the table. "Please go and grab a wrap for our friend."

Antonia disappeared deferentially as Tía Margarita dipped a crumpet in the dog's tea and then fed him tiny nibbles. "Fernando," she said to her grand-nephew, "why don't you show Jessica outside and into the sunshine?"

"She's not related by blood," he said with a wink.

Jess hadn't initially considered the ramifications, but now that he'd mentioned it, maybe she was glad. Not that having an eccentric old person in the family really mattered most of the time. If they lived long enough, most folks probably turned that way, even without trying.

"She was married to your uncle?"

"Great-uncle, that's right."

"At first, the family felt it a shame they never had children. Then, after a while…" He shrugged and shot her a wry smile. "Oh my, imagine that!" he said, leaning toward her and fingering her hair.

"What is it?" she asked with alarm.

He gazed in her eyes in a way that brought back tumbling meadows. "When your hair holds the sun, it looks like gold." He grinned and pulled something from his pocket. "And gold…is of such beauty, it deserves to be prominently displayed. Don't you agree?"

Jess gasped in surprise as he held that marvelous pair of earrings in her direction and lifted them up to one ear. "Very nice," he said with a satisfied smile. "They suit you."

He laid the pair in her palm, then watched her expectantly, apparently hoping he'd gotten this right. Fernando had more than gotten this right; in one deft move, he'd nearly blown her away. Jess felt as if her heart might burst open and tears spring from her eyes at the same time. Nobody had ever done anything like this for her before.

"But how did you know?" she asked, her voice hoarse with emotion.

"I have my sources at the monastery." He stepped closer.

A tear trickled down her cheek. "They're wonderful."

"Then why are you crying?" he asked with a worried frown.

"Because you really are a marvelous man." Before she knew what she was doing, Jess had wrapped her arms around his neck and was up on her tiptoes, kissing him.

He pulled her close and returned her fire with one glorious bout of passion after the next. Jess lost track of time and culture and continent. All she knew was that she was with her hunky matador man who brought her gifts of the heart. How could he be so solid yet giving at once?

"Teatime!" Tía Margarita called, loudly tinkling a bell.

Fernando released Jessica with a hearty laugh.

"Terribly sorry, Tía Margarita," he said, obviously not meaning it.

Tía Margarita toddled toward the table, waving her lace hanky in the air.

"Young people!" she said to Rudolfo, who was making his way around the table, lapping at all the plates.

Jess slipped the leather bookmark from its bag and placed it on the nightstand beside the old Bible. It had been half her lifetime since she'd cracked the good book. Faith really hadn't gotten her anywhere, so she'd given it up as years went by. Though there had been a time when she'd found some point in it. As a hopeful teen, she'd spent hours poring over the same passage in Corinthians, wistfully dreaming up what true love might mean. She wondered if she could still find it. It couldn't be that difficult. Sort of like riding a bicycle, right?

The door creaked open, and Fernando stuck his head in.

"Oh, sorry!" he said. "I thought you were downstairs."

After their return from town, Ana María had spent quite a bit of time introducing her new daughter-in-law to the contents of her hope chest. Fernando had begged off the moment the baby fashion show had started. He likely felt guilty he'd let things go so far but didn't have the guts at that moment to rain on his mom's parade. Of course Jess could understand that. Ana María had appeared so expressive and glowing, commenting on the joys of impending grandchildren, that Jess hadn't had the heart to break the bad news either.

"Wait, are you reading the Bible?"

Jess stared down at the tome in her hand, fretfully embarrassed. "Not really," she said, snapping it shut. "Just thinking of where to put the bookmark."

"Genesis?" he retorted with one raised eyebrow.

"The beginning, yes!" she said, nervously fumbling through brittle pages. Locating Genesis shouldn't be *that* difficult. *On the first day…* Thank God! She slid the bookmark inside, then glanced heavenward, fearful she'd committed some sort of mental blasphemy.

"I was just coming for my things," Fernando said. "All right if I grab a pillow?"

"What?" Jess asked weakly, almost wishing she hadn't started this God thing. Now she worried that the heavenly angels were watching them. Maybe had been watching them all along. She felt instantly consumed by heat, thinking the Catholicism was getting to her.

"It's nearly eleven. I thought I'd take what I needed for bed."

What about what *she* needed for bed? That clearly wasn't Fernando scooping up his things and waltzing out of here. Not after today, not after that kiss. *Not after our lovemaking this morning either,* she thought, quickly covering the Bible with the monastery bag.

"Fernando," she said as coolly as she could manage. "Your mother just spent two hours expounding on the joys of grandparenthood. Don't you think it would seem odd for you to spend the night downstairs?"

He brought his hand to his chin and, in all seriousness, considered this. "You're right," he said, leveling a gaze at her. "We pulled that last night. Doesn't really seem right to try it again."

She shook her head in accord. "Not so soon, anyway."

"Then you won't mind if I stay here?"

"We're still married for now," she said, giving a little laugh.

Fernando suspiciously eyed the bag-covered Bible. "In the eyes of the church."

Jess mustered her best stern expression. "We can't go disappointing your mom."

"She's bound to be heartbroken soon enough," he agreed.

"So, we're still going to Seville tomorrow?" she asked a little sadly.

"That *is* what you want?"

His gaze locked on hers and was so penetratingly hot she felt as if he'd stripped all her clothes off. That *was* what she wanted, wasn't it? To unmarry this guy?

Fernando stepped into the room and locked the door behind him.

"Yes," she said uncertainly. "Yes, of course."

"Then, we'll go to Seville," he said, unbuttoning his shirt. He let it slide from his broad shoulders as he walked toward the bed with catlike stealth, every…single…muscle under control. "In the morning."

Chapter Eight

Fernando stretched out his arms for Jess in the empty bed. *Gone? She can't possibly be gone.* He opened his eyes in a panic to spy her simple white shift still hanging in the open armoire. Relief flooded him as he sent his attention to the bathroom. The door was ajar, yet he heard nothing. Fernando sat up and stared at the clock as five minutes ticked by. Then ten. Something seemed amiss. "Jessica?" he called gently. "*Querida?*"

Nothing.

Fernando rose from the bed and walked toward the bath with purposeful strides, his heart pounding. Through the crack in the door, he spied her curled up in a ball on the floor, her arms crossed over her head.

"Jessica," he said, kneeling by her. "Darling, what's wrong?"

"I don't think I'm going to Seville," came the weak reply.

"Well, then, that settles it," he said in an attempt to reassure her. "I'm not going either."

Her skin was as pale as her nightgown, and she shivered slightly. On the simple throw rug on top of the cold tile, she was bound to be freezing.

"Are you sick?" he asked with concern.

She nodded, shielding her eyes against the light streaming in through the window.

"My stomach."

Fernando thought of the caldo they'd had last night in town as well as the vast array of *tapas*. None of it had affected him. Then again, his stomach was made of steel.

"I'm calling a doctor," he said, decisively.

"No…don't."

"Jessica," he stated reasonably. "You can't even get off the floor. If you have food poisoning, I think that—"

"It wasn't the food, Fernando," she said, glancing up at him all squinty-eyed. It pained him immensely to see her this way. "I'm just not feeling well."

"What can I get you?" he asked, believing that no request could be too great.

"All I need is rest."

She looked like her death, and he couldn't stand it. "It's not good for you to be lying on the floor. Let me help you back to the bed." He laid his hand on her arm and found it chilled. "Come on," he pleaded sincerely, "please let me help you."

He held out his hands, and she accepted his grip as he pulled her gently upright. "Here," he said, steadying her against his side as he sheltered her with one arm, "lean against me. We'll be there in no time."

She clambered into bed and moaned as he tucked her under the covers. Fernando felt utterly helpless. He'd never seen Jessica so debilitated. The woman he knew was capable and strong. To see her like this was crushing. "Has this happened to you before?"

"I don't get sick, Fernando," she answered defensively, even though her ailing tone gave her away. Just as she didn't fall in love, he pondered, recalling her earlier statement. Here was a woman who allowed herself no weakness.

"You don't always have to be strong with me," he said, sitting on his side of the bed. "None of us can be strong always."

"Not even matadors?" she asked.

"Not even matadors," he assured her with a tender smile. "We bruise as easily as telecommunications experts.

In some ways, maybe more. When you're trained to be tough on the outside, it's hard to allow feelings in. Then when you do, I'm afraid, they can hurt twice as much if they betray you."

She didn't answer but was quiet and listened. Maybe being in bed was starting to help. He lay down next to her and nestled her in his arms, spooning her back against his chest.

"Is it all right if I hold you?" he asked hoarsely, hoping she wouldn't protest.

She snuggled back against him in response, and he tightened his arms around her. As he did, his hand brushed her cheek and found it damp. She was crying.

"Everything's going to be fine," he said, lightly kissing her shoulder. "Don't worry, *querida*. Seville will still be there tomorrow."

That was precisely what broke her heart. Seville wouldn't just be there tomorrow. It would also be there the day after, and the next. Sooner or later, Jess and Fernando would go to Seville, meet with the magistrate, and clear up the paperwork. Then, she'd be back to her ordinary life in America. The one she'd grown accustomed to and which she'd once believed had suited her so well. No one in her life who'd loved her had ever stayed. And now here was someone who adored her, and she was running away. She didn't know why Fernando had become so taken with her, but she now trusted in his sincerity when he said he had. Why else would he be willing to let her go, unless that was what he believed she needed for her own happiness?

Jess let the tears quietly fall as she recalled tumbling meadows and the innocence of childhood. There'd been a time when she'd believed in the beauty in this world and had trusted in those who protected her not to hurt her. Jess honestly wasn't prone to illness and barely ever missed a day at work. However, there'd been one time when she was fifteen that she hadn't been able to get out of bed for two weeks.

"Do you know what he said to me?" Jess said softly.

"Who?" Fernando asked.

"My father, when he left."

"No, what did he say?"

"He said…" She caught her breath but kept crying, the tears pouring harder. "He said, 'It's good you've learned love's an illusion now. It will save you lots of heartache in the future.'"

"Oh, Jessica. My dear Jessica… Your father was wrong, so very wrong to say that."

Her voice was a whimper now, her shoulders lightly rocking with her sobs. "He left me and my mom and never looked back. Not one card. Not one phone call. I don't even know where he went."

Fernando tightened his grip around her, desperately longing to keep her safe. Defended from her past and protected from an uncertain future. He'd provide a future with anything she wanted, if only she could give him her heart.

"Some men are like that," he said with a bitter edge to his voice. "And I'm sorry. Sorry on behalf of all of them. But Jessica," he said, hugging her to him. "You've got to believe that not all of us are."

"I know," she said between sobs.

Fernando held her firmly, not knowing what else he could say or do. And then, after a bit, the crying lessened, and it seemed she was drifting off to sleep.

"Can we just stay here awhile?" she asked, beginning to doze.

"For as long as you'd like," he said, holding her close.

Ana María entered the kitchen as Fernando was grilling a *pan tostado*.

"Making your own breakfast?" Ana María asked with surprise. "Consuelo will be down any minute."

"I didn't want to trouble Consuelo," Fernando answered, putting the kettle to boil.

"What's going on?" his mother asked suspiciously.

"Jessica's not feeling well."

"Oh dear!" she said with alarm. And then with a knowing nod, she added, "Ah, the morning sickness. It's begun already."

"Isn't it early?" Fernando asked.

"Depends on the woman, as well as the pregnancy," Ana María stated with authority. "With Margarita, I didn't feel it for months. With you, however, I was sick right away. I chalked it up to conflicting hormones."

Fernando felt a flash of pride at the thought of fathering a boy. Though a little girl would be nice too. He stopped himself, realizing he was fantasizing about a pregnancy that didn't exist. "Mamá, about the baby... I don't think we should get too carried away or excited."

"Posh! Babies are always exciting. Such joys. Just you wait and see, Fernando, when you hold your own child in your arms."

He had to admit the thought of having a baby had its appeal, particularly with one beautiful blonde as the mother. She'd look just like the Madonna, with her halo of golden hair. He'd never suspected she was so religious until he'd caught her reading the Bible.

"Fernando, your toast is burning," she warned as smoke curled from the oven.

He hastily withdrew the tray, seeing from its charred contents he'd have to start over.

"Perhaps you should let Consuelo bring it up after all?" his mother suggested.

"Maybe you're right," he answered, thinking he'd been away from his Madonna too long. What if she awakened and missed having him there?

"I wonder if he'll have blue eyes," Ana María said. "Or green, like yours?"

"Who?"

"Your son, of course."

"Mother," he said seriously. "I need to talk to you about the baby—and the marriage too."

Her cheeks sagged with concern. "What's happened, Fernando?"

"It's maybe what hasn't," he said, hanging his head.

Ana María righted his chin in her hands. "I'm your mother. You can tell me."

"You'll be disappointed," he said, unable to meet her eyes.

"Do you love her?"

"What?"

"Fernando, look at me."

He met her warm brown gaze, laced with compassion.

"I said," she repeated softly, "do you love her?"

"With my whole heart, Mamá."

"Then, you don't need to tell me the details. You're a grown man, and whatever the problem is, I trust that you will fix it."

"What if I can't?"

She slapped him across the chest, causing him to take a step back in surprise. "Are you a mouse or a man? What happened to the tough little boy who wanted to take on the bulls, eh? That boy," she said, placing a hand on her hip, "is still in there. Being gored by a bull once didn't take him away."

Fernando admired his mother's brutal beauty. She was, without question, as tough as any beast he'd ever faced.

"I understand what you have sacrificed for me. I know you left the ring because you didn't want to leave me a widow and the mother of a dead child besides. But your heart was there. You loved the sport and were extremely skilled at it too. Maybe even more talented than your grandfather. You were never afraid for yourself, only concerned for me. And now, I am concerned for you. You have to fight for your life, Fernando. Fight for the life you want and the one you believe in your heart you were born to have."

He stared at her a long while, swallowing hard. He never could have made it in this world without her. Of all the attributes she possessed, her wisdom was her greatest strength. She was right, of course. About everything.

"Thanks, Mother," he said, feeling the heat in his eyes but keeping emotions at bay. "I will take your advice to heart."

Jess stumbled across the room, still half dazed from her deep slumber. That infernal telephone had rung half a dozen times—then a pause—then it would start up again! Following the chime and its accompanying vibration, she lurched for a chair beside the picture window onto which Fernando had hastily dropped his trousers last night. Something jiggled and jumped just beneath the open fly. Ah! She grabbed for the cell just in time, midway between ring three and four.

"Please tell me you're in Seville."

"Evie?" Jess said with surprise. "What are you doing calling me here?"

"I had the number from your incoming call. What do you think?"

Jess pushed Fernando's slacks aside, sat in the chair, and rubbed her brow. "I think it's nine in the morning. What's your point?"

"My point is, I just woke up with the most horrible nightmare. I had visions of you telling me the whole trip was off."

"What trip?" Jess said, feigning innocence.

"To Seville, you big dummy!"

"It is off," Jess said. "But not like you think."

"I don't get what you're saying."

"I'm saying I need to spend the day in bed."

"Jess…" Evie said, her voice pitched low, "now's not the time to turn into a sex machine."

"A what? No! You don't understand. I have a headache."

"What?"

"And a stomach ache too. Really, my tummy's killing me."

"You never get sick."

"I know. That's the kicker."

There was an odd pause at the other end of the line.

"Where's the matador?" Evie finally said.

Jess panned the room, peering into the bathroom as well.

"Honestly, I don't know."

"Good. Then you can tell me the truth."

"I just did."

"You're playing possum, Jess."

Jess sat up a little straighter, indignant. "I take offense at what you're saying."

"I thought you told me there was some sort of timeline going on here."

"Well… Maybe."

"That you had to get to the magistrate to stop him from sending the paperwork to Madrid."

Jess's eyes fell on the Bible, midway across the room. "We're still married in the eyes of the church."

"Now you're talking crazy."

Jess heard whistling in the hall and knew Fernando was coming. He pressed open the door, carrying a plentiful tray. "Breakfast is served!" he said with a flourish. His eyes fell on hers as she frantically gripped the phone.

"Jess!" Evie yelped.

"Gotta dash!" Jess said, quickly hitting End Call.

"Who was that?" Fernando asked, setting the tray on a table.

"Only my very best friend on earth, Evie."

"Splendid," he said with a smile. "She'll have to come and visit."

Eve shoved garments into her carry-on bag, the one that could easily fit into the overhead compartments on airplanes. Jessica Bloom had totally flipped her lid, and Eve was going to have to fly to Iberia to unflip it. Jesus H. Christ. She was under a tight deadline at work, and her bosses would be furious at her for skipping out on them now. What could she say to take leave on such short notice? Maybe that a close relative had died? Yes, that would work. Besides, it was nearly the truth. The girl she'd known and loved since middle school had turned into a virtual stranger.

Eve set the coffeepot to brew and started searching airlines on the Internet. She couldn't get a travel deal through an online retailer at the last minute. She'd have to book the flight directly. Maybe the dead-relative ruse would work with them as well. That might even give her a discount. She was going to get Jess for this, she surely was.

Jess was the most cynical person Eve knew. She didn't even believe in love. So how come all of a sudden she seemed all bent on getting stuck in a marriage? Perhaps the matador was wicked or had cast some kind of weird spell over her. Eve had heard there were gypsies in Spain. Could they have gotten involved somehow with some sort of black magic?

Eve twisted up her hair and shoved a chopstick into the knot. She'd had carry-out last night for dinner but had been lazy and used a fork, so this one was clean. She felt a rash coming on, her skin getting all itchy, and thought maybe she'd better take an antihistamine. Eve wondered briefly if she should call Jess's mother, then decided against it on two counts. One, it was three in the morning, and two, Jess's mom was a little high-strung to start. No sense in stringing her out further, when maybe there wasn't much to worry about. *Like hell,* Eve thought; there was plenty to worry about. But that was her job as the best friend. She was smart. She had a skill set. She even spoke Spanish! Much better than Jess, for crying out loud. And Jess was the one who'd bought into some bull. *Okay, calm down, Eve,* she told herself. *Spinning off into about a billion directions won't do. Make a list, that's right. Starting with email to bosses.*

Eve felt a stab of panic, wondering what she'd do if Jess wouldn't cooperate once she got there. You couldn't call Child Protective Services on someone over eighteen, and they probably wouldn't help if that party was in another country anyway. It didn't matter. Eve could figure the rest of it out once she got to La Esperanza del Corazón and had studied the situation firsthand. Clearly, when Jess saw her face-to-face, she'd realize how out of touch with reality she'd become and beg Eve to take her home. It was hard being the responsible one in the relationship. That was normally Jess's job, but she'd somehow turned the tables on Eve. And Eve didn't like it one bit.

Jess and Fernando sat in bed, snacking on the remains of their "light" breakfast.

"I'm glad to see you're feeling so much better," Fernando said.

"Yes, thanks. The tea instead of coffee was a good move. Though, don't get me wrong. I totally love the coffee here. Just not today," she said, polishing off her toast.

She really had quite a good appetite once she got started. They'd had to have Consuelo bring up extra biscuits and tea—twice.

"I'm glad that you talked to me," he said sincerely. "About what was bothering you before."

She surveyed him, brilliant blue eyes smiling. "You know what they say, confession is good for the soul."

"Are you Catholic?" he asked suddenly.

"No. Methodist. Why?"

"It's nothing. I just wondered."

"I would have to convert, wouldn't I?"

"What do you mean?"

"Isn't there some kind of rule about that? About Protestants marrying Catholics?"

"I'd have to look it up," he said.

"Now you're teasing me."

"I don't believe anyone should do anything that they don't want to. Concerning religion or anything else. I understand that you hold your own beliefs."

She shot him a curious glance. "Fernando," she said, "what's going to happen when we get to Seville?"

"Anything you'd like. Why?"

"You know what I'm talking about—the magistrate."

"Yes, well, of course we'll go there. That's on the agenda."

"Agenda?" she asked, staring up at him with big, innocent eyes.

"There's a lot to see in Sevilla, Jessica. Given that you may never go there again, I'd hate for you not to take full advantage of the trip."

"What are you suggesting?"

"Only one thing."

She waited expectantly.

"That before we go to the magistrate, you allow me to show you something."

"Like...?" she pressed.

"Just something," he said, holding firm.

There was plenty he intended to show her. Given her devout nature, starting with the Cathedral of Seville. Then there'd be a long walk by the river. Perhaps a lazy lunch in the Barrio de Santa Cruz... Oh! He'd forgotten the Giralda, a lovely Moorish tower adjoining the Cathedral and once belonging to the ancient mosque that had previously stood in its place. There was also the Tower of Gold, the Archives of the Indies, the Royal Alcazar...

"All right," she agreed, "but how long will that take?"

"That's hard to say," he offered. "Better pack an overnight bag."

Chapter Nine

Jess didn't have a whole lot to put in an overnight bag. When she'd run off with Fernando to La Esperanza del Corazón, she'd left most of her things in the business apartment in Madrid. She'd been flying back and forth so frequently, the home office had set her up with a semipermanent spot. The neat little efficiency apartment was a short walk to Retiro Park and a block from the Prado, not that she often had time to take in the sights during her hurried business trips. There were so many meetings to attend, with principle players and corporate affiliates all vying for her attention. Global Financial Telecom was in the *come home to papa* business, and everyone in the industry knew it. Smaller entities absorbed by GFT were favored by a worldwide reach and saw their stock values double overnight. Jess didn't really mind being in the takeover business when the other parties were all so eager to jump. Besides, she'd enjoyed the people she'd met, all of whom were intelligent and interesting. Only one had been devastatingly handsome, and had made her heart skip a beat each time he'd met her eyes with his piercing green gaze.

While she never let on, the truth was that, over time, Jess increasingly looked forward to her little jaunts to Madrid. She and Fernando didn't just converse, they verbally jousted. And she'd found herself more aroused, and her interest more piqued, by each sparring encounter. He just may have been trying to talk up his firm's market price, but he did so in a way that Jess found unbearably enticing. She'd never seen a wedding band and had heard rumors on both sides of the Atlantic about the ultra-eligible man being single. Still, she never would have considered making a move. That simply wasn't her. Besides, how messy that would be, becoming involved with a business colleague who lived an ocean away! Given her abysmal track record with men, anything more than a simple flirtation wasn't worth the risk. Now, she was married. *Married.*

Jess folded her cream-colored slacks in half and tucked them in her bag. Given the pitcher of sangria or two she'd downed in preparation, it seemed stunningly prescient that she'd packed a wardrobe exclusively in shades of white. She hadn't known straightaway they were going to La Esperanza del Corazón to get hitched. Fernando had asked her only two questions. One, did she feel like doing something wild. And two, would she like to see where he came from. Both sounded unbelievably reckless and exciting. They left late-night voice mails to their respective offices saying Jess was touring the south with Fernando to evaluate some of his business holdings. In a way, that had been true, Jess decided, thinking of the vineyard.

Why Fernando had whisked her into town and wanted to show her that little church courtyard in the middle of the night, she couldn't anticipate. It seemed as if he hadn't totally planned it either. Because his bumping into Father Domingo there had appeared a legitimate surprise. Not half an hour later, Fernando was asking her to marry him, and she'd be damned if, at that moment, it didn't seem exactly right. He was so handsome standing there in the moonlight. And when he held her and made her promises... Jess felt her knees weaken at the memory of that very first time. She was glad she'd had the foresight to pack several nighties, two of which she tossed in her suitcase now.

Jess stared down at the heap of clothes in her bag, thinking it didn't precisely look like she was packing for an annulment. She gingerly dangled a white silk thong from one finger, considering whether she should take it back out. That could depend entirely on what she anticipated might happen on this trip. Jess dug through her larger bag until she found several more skimpy undergarments, deciding to bring them along. Truth was, none of these items took up much space. One way or another, it was best to be prepared.

Fernando steadied his arms around her and nestled her back against his chest as she gazed at the panorama. "So what do you think?" he whispered in her ear.

"It's stunning," she said, still a bit breathless from the steep climb up the numerous ramps.

They stood at the pinnacle of La Giralda, the original minaret from the old Moorish mosque that once stood in the place of Seville's enormous cathedral. Rumor held that when the Catholics drove the Moors from Spain, they'd razed everything connected to Islam, save a few lovely relics they'd found too abundantly beautiful to destroy. There was the Alhambra Palace in Granada, the famed mosque in Córdoba, and this charming tower here, which the Catholics had bastardized by transforming the place once used for calling Muslims to prayer into a bell tower aimed at beckoning Catholics to mass.

It was a warm and sunny afternoon, a comfortable glow settling over the ancient part of the city and the whitewashed former Jewish Quarter flanking La Giralda's edge. All afternoon, they'd meandered cobblestoned streets, stopping here and there for a chilled white sherry or a pitcher of sangria, with small rations of snacks, or *tapas*, offered on the side. Fernando had checked them into a nice hotel with a lovely courtyard behind a wrought-iron gate, stating it was never wise to do business in Seville in the afternoon. Seeing a magistrate was best reserved for the severity of morning, before people had enjoyed their midday meal, a nice bottle of wine, and the accompanying *siesta*. With him being the local and all, and more familiar with the landscape, Jess had naturally decided to defer to his judgment. They clearly couldn't have some magistrate mucking things up on account of a good Rioja.

Fernando pointed out other landmarks around them, including the buildings of a more modern Seville across the waters of the Guadalquivir, and the remnants of an ancient maritime fortress situated on this side of its banks.

"I thought tonight we'd take in a flamenco show," he told her.

"But we saw one of those in Madrid."

"Imposters!" he declared with a laugh. "Flamenco comes from the south. It's a blend of historical regional dance influenced by our Moorish cousins. What you saw in Madrid is adequate but for the tourists. What I'll take you to here, you'll also see children dance in the streets, especially at Feria."

"Feria?"

"It's the big festival in the spring, connected to the sherry harvest. You'd love it, I think."

She gazed back at him over her shoulder, captivated by hypnotic green eyes.

"There are lots of horses…" he tempted.

"Why are you so sure I like horses?"

"Because," he said, giving her a little squeeze, "I've seen how you ride."

"Oh? How's that?"

"Like a woman who was born to the saddle," he said, giving her neck a kiss.

A group of school children had paraded onto the parapet. A couple pointed and giggled at Fernando's public display of affection while their teacher scorched them with a disapproving glare.

"Come on," he said, breaking away and taking her hand. "Let's go have a late lunch."

"And think about taking a siesta?" she asked hopefully.

"Absolutely," he said with a grin.

Eve gawked as the cabbie pulled through the gate of the expansive hacienda.

"Are you sure we're in the right place?"

"Casa Garcia de la Vega, *sí.*"

"Maybe we've got the wrong one."

"There's only one family in town with that name."

He came to a halt at the height of the circular drive between a flowering rose garden and an imposing front door. For the first time since she'd book her Iberia flight, Eve felt a sense of panic. What if she'd done the wrong thing in coming here? What if these people were lunatics and stocked the place like a fortress with knives and guns? Even worse, what if they were terribly good people, high-bred and well-mannered, and Jess became furious at her for becoming involved? Eve swallowed hard and stepped from the cab, thinking it was no time to chicken out now.

She rapped three times, and, after what seemed like an eternity, an old man in dirty britches and holding garden tools answered. "*Bueno?*" he said by way of greeting.

"Ah yes," she answered in crisp, clear Castilian. Eve was very proud of herself for being the first one in her class in Spanish Four. The fact that this had been in high school didn't diminish the fact. "I was hoping to find Ms. Jessica Bloom at home."

He lowered his brow and stared at her. "*No existe.*"

She didn't exist? Oh my God! They had killed her! Eve frantically glanced around, wishing with all her might she'd asked the taxi driver to wait. Here she was, a million miles from nowhere, with the gardener from some maniac family holding murderous shears. She stared down at his hedge clippers, thinking she spied hints of dried blood. Maybe it was red Spanish clay. She wasn't sure but certainly wasn't ready to take the chance. Eve took two giant steps back, nearly stumbling down the stone stairs.

The old man surveyed her cautiously, then began to close the door.

"Pedrito!" a woman's voice called from inside. "Who's there?"

The man stepped aside, his keen eye on Eve, almost like he believed her to be the dangerous party.

"Hello," the elegant middle-aged woman said. "I'm Ana María Garcia de la Vega. How may I help you?"

"I'm Eve. Eve Parker," she said, extending her hand.

Ana María shook it, appearing vaguely uncomfortable with the gesture.

"You come from America?"

"In search of my friend, Jessica Bloom. Last I heard, she was here."

Ana María smiled pleasantly. "She's a Garcia de la Vega now."

"So I heard," Eve said, willing herself to remain calm.

"And yes, she was here, but I'm afraid she's not now. She and Fernando have gone to Seville."

"Thank God!" Eve cried, unable to stop herself. She cupped her hand to her mouth, recalling she was in a very Catholic country.

Ana María shared a disapproving look. "They've gone there on holiday. Their honeymoon."

"Honeymoon?"

"What else might one assume? They've only been married five days."

Eve hoped Ana María had it wrong. Surely she meant they'd gone there to get an annulment. But if Ana María didn't know that, Eve decided she ought not to mention it. The concept of slaying the messenger was common to all lands, and there was a man holding sharp implements nearby.

"Can you point me in the direction of Seville?" Eve smiled brightly and acted like she asked the question every day.

Ana María studied her for a prolonged beat. "Are Jessica and Fernando expecting you?"

"Jess is like a sister to me." And then, thinking quickly, she added. "I want nothing more than to congratulate the happy couple. I come bearing a wedding gift!"

As proof, she pulled two Iberia boarding passes from her purse and flashed them in Ana María's direction, much too quickly for her to make out any details.

"After all, why honeymoon in Seville when your very best friend on earth treats you to the romantic vacation of a lifetime in Paris?"

Ana María's expression softened. "Oh, how lovely. What a very good friend you must be."

"I only want what's best for Jess," Eve said, nodding solemnly. "For Jess and Fernando."

"Well, then, of course I'll point you in the direction of Seville. Better than that, I'll have my driver take you."

Eve's chest constricted at the thought of being out on the desolate Iberian plains with the butcher of Seville.

"Oh no, really. I wouldn't trouble you—or him."

"It's no trouble," a gorgeous hunk said, stepping from around the corner. "Hello," he said with dark sexy eyes and a knock-your-socks-off smile. "I'm Gustavo, and I'm free for the afternoon."

Eve swallowed her tongue and stopped herself from asking what he was doing tonight.

"Gustavo is our darling Consuelo's son, very reliable and an excellent driver."

"Well, if you insist," Eve said, feeling as if she were turning the color of a very ripe plum.

"Of course I insist," Ana María said with a kind smile. "But first, dear, please do come in, refresh yourself a bit, and have a spot of tea."

Chapter Ten

"Wait! Pull over. I think that's them," Eve yelped, causing Gustavo to bring the elegant sedan to a halt on the busy boulevard. Other drivers honked and shouted insults.

"Are you sure?" Gustavo asked.

Eve leaned out her window and shouted to the blonde seated on a bench by the river. "Jess!" Her back was to them, but she was with a man, a very handsome man. They were both laughing and eating ice cream. "Jessica Bloom! Is that you?"

Jess swiveled her head in surprise as Fernando turned to stare.

"That's Fernando, all right," Gustavo said, steering their car onto the curb.

"Evie?" Jess asked in shock as Eve bolted from the car.

"Thank God you're okay!" Eve said, rushing to her.

Jess stood uncertainly as Eve pulled her into her arms.

"Evie," Jess said in disbelief. "What are you doing here?"

Gustavo approached at an even gait.

"Gustavo?" Fernando said sternly. "What's going on?"

"Your mother asked me to bring her to Seville," Gustavo said, indicating Eve.

"Fernando," Jess said in wonderment. "This is Eve Parker, my very best friend."

"Evie!" Fernando said, stunning Eve by sweeping her into his arms. "I told Jess to invite you to visit!"

"You did?" Eve asked, taken aback.

"But I never imagined you'd act so fast!" He gave her two swift pecks on the cheeks. "Ah yes, you're just as Jess described. Beautiful and capable." In spite of herself, Eve felt herself blush. "We're so pleased you could come. Aren't we, Jessica?"

But Jess just stared at Eve slack-jawed. Fernando undoubtedly was eye candy with that adorable smile and his rock-hard six-pack. His formfitting polo did nothing to disguise the phenomenal physique beneath it. Maybe he'd hypnotized Jess with his undulating abs.

A siren blared, and the group turned to see a police officer approaching.

"Maybe we should move the car off the curb?" Gustavo suggested.

Jess sat in the backseat, unsure if she was happy to see Evie or whether she was fuming. The truth was, Evie showing up this way had completely caught her off guard. Fernando had seemed to take it in stride, welcoming her good-naturedly to their little gathering. Jess had caught only a glimpse of Gustavo at the house once. She hadn't observed how good-looking he was until she'd seen him up close. She wondered if Evie had noticed, then decided she didn't particularly care. She was irritated with Evie right now. Way irritated. She and Fernando had tickets to a rare exhibit at the *Archivo General de Indias* tonight. There was to be champagne and live music and the unveiling of some "Discovery of the New World" documents not yet revealed to the general public. Jess was living and breathing history here, and it was exhilarating. She felt like an explorer, and Fernando Garcia de la Vega was her sexy conquistador.

"That bring back memories, Fernando?" Gustavo asked as they swung around the Plaza de Toros de la Real Maestranza de Caballería de Sevilla, the oldest and most famous bullring in Spain.

"None that I care to remember."

"Fernando's just being modest," Gustavo told the ladies. "Fernando was a very fine matador in his day. He could have gone on to be one of Spain's best."

"Gustavo's exaggerating."

"No, he's not," Evie butted in. "I ran a search on him. Gustavo's right."

Gustavo glanced at Evie while Fernando uncomfortably cleared his throat.

"Where are we going?" Fernando asked.

"I was hoping you'd tell me." Gustavo shrugged. "I just work here."

Fernando shot Jess a questioning look.

"Don't ask me. I didn't even know she was coming."

"What?" Fernando asked as Gustavo focused on driving nowhere, minding his own business.

Evie bristled a bit in the front seat. "I thought you'd be happy to see me," she told Jess.

"Of course I'm happy," Jess said, fighting the confusion racing through her heart and head. "You just surprised me, that's all."

"How about we stop for some fish and chips?" Gustavo offered brightly.

"Great thought, Gustavo! I know the best place for fresh fried calamari," he told the girls.

Gustavo held up an authoritative finger. "And *croquetas*. Don't forget the *croquetas*."

"They go great with Spanish beer," Fernando said, trying to read the worry on Jess's face.

"But the *Archivo*?" she asked weakly. This whole Evie thing really had her undone. It wasn't that she didn't love her best friend. But it would have been polite for Evie to have at least called ahead.

"Don't worry, *mi amor*," Fernando said, kissing her hand. "We'll get there another time."

Jess caught Evie studying them suspiciously in the rearview mirror.

"How did things go at the magistrate?"

Fernando pursed his lips and stared out the window, reassuringly patting Jess's hand.

"Um…" Jess began. "We've been meaning to go. I mean, it's on the agenda." Even in the reflective glass she could see Evie's expression darkening. "But, in all honestly, there hasn't been time."

"It's true," Fernando leapt in. "Things have been busy."

"Very busy," Jess repeated unnecessarily.

"There's a lot to see in Seville," Gustavo added, trying to be helpful.

Evie glared at him, obviously resenting the intrusion.

"How long have you been in Seville?" she asked, turning toward Jess.

"Two, no three…?" She tilted her head at Fernando.

"Three days," he said with a love-sick smile. "It all blurs together somehow."

Gustavo raised his brow and kept on driving, while Evie felt sick to her stomach. This was far worse than she imagined. Jess had apparently hypnotized the matador too!

Evie kicked herself for not coming up with a full-scale plan before she got here. She saw now she was wrong to think Jess would be thrilled to see her, would rush into her arms, all tears, and say *best friend on earth, pretty please, take me home.* She needed to get Jess alone and talk to her; that was what she needed to do. Just the two of them, no sexy Spaniards involved. She glanced at Gustavo, and he gave her a crooked smile, causing her heart to beat faster. The men here were dangerous. It was easy enough to see that. No way could Jess think clearly when she was caught up in all of this. Somehow, some way, Eve was going to get

Jess alone tonight and talk some sense into her. Then tomorrow, they'd go to the magistrate. All of them. Together. There'd be no more taking chances with this one. Eve just hoped it wasn't already too late.

Fernando worried over the sudden appearance of Jess's best friend. Though she wore a smile, something in his gut told him that Eve Parker wasn't here to congratulate them. She was here to tell Jessica she'd made a mistake and encourage her to return to America. He hoisted his beer and took another swig as the group eagerly dug into fried fish and Gustavo regaled them with funny stories. Surely the woman he'd fallen in love with wasn't that malleable. She'd know her own mind, wouldn't she, and stand up for what she felt in her heart? The problem was, she'd not yet confessed those emotions to Fernando. Though he'd sensed her getting closer to admitting her feelings to him, she still kept them somewhat guarded.

Fernando was sure Jessica was the woman for him and certain he'd eventually be able to convince her. All he needed was the gift of time. The two of them were well suited, meant for each other. Jessica needed a man who was strong enough to stand by his word to honor and protect her, and he needed a woman he could nurture and who could benefit from his strength. He longed to help and take care of her, to support her in developing any sort of career that she wished, while she became the woman he knew she so longed to be. Someone comfortable with herself and completely self-assured. Secure in the knowledge that someone truly loved her…and would never let her go.

Fernando reached beside him to take Jessica's hand. She let him hold it briefly, then casually withdrew it, wrapping her fingers around the chilled glass holding her beer. "That's right!" she said to Eve. "I remember!"

They both laughed companionably, sharing memories of some happy event Fernando had missed in his brooding. The distancing had already begun. The woman before him had transformed from his loving new wife into someone he scarcely knew. But if Jessica could be so easily dissuaded from her growing feelings for Fernando, perhaps there existed more of a chasm between them than Fernando had imagined to begin with.

"What are the plans from here?" Gustavo prompted as a waiter cleared the table.

"I suppose I'll need to talk to Jessica about that," Fernando answered. He noted she averted her gaze even as he spoke.

"He's right," Jessica told the group. "Fernando and I will need to talk."

"Where are you staying?" Eve asked.

Jessica glanced at Fernando. "In the Barrio de Santa Cruz."

"Perhaps we should stay there too," Eve said.

Gustavo was pleasantly intrigued. "I couldn't possibly leave you here without a driver."

"In two rooms, I meant," she said, shooting Gustavo a look.

He clutched his hands to his chest, feigning heartbreak. "You can't blame a man for hoping."

In spite of himself, Fernando chuckled. Having been raised in the same house, Gustavo hadn't only been a boyhood friend. He was the closest thing Fernando had to a brother.

Eve blushed and flagrantly batted her eyes at Gustavo. "That doesn't mean I won't go out for sangria later…"

"You have to watch it with that sangria," Jessica said.

Fernando met her gaze and held it. "Very dangerous, I hear."

Chapter Eleven

"Are you interested in Gustavo?" Jess asked as Eve hung three items in her closet. Evie never traveled with more than three items. Mix and match, with assorted colored T-shirts and accessories. Her weekend wardrobe. She'd read somewhere in a magazine that this was how one got away with packing light. For someone who rarely traveled, she'd really taken the advice to heart.

"A woman would have to be blind not to be interested in Gustavo," she said. "But that's not why I'm letting him take me out for drinks."

Jess narrowed her eyes, reading her best friend. "You want me to talk to Fernando, don't you? To tell him tomorrow we're going to the magistrate and that this marriage is off."

"Isn't that what you want?" Evie asked her reasonably. "Listen, Jess. I understand Fernando's beautiful. Maybe even nice, and very, very rich."

"Wow, you're making him sound like a cad."

"Don't get snippy on me, pretty please. Stop for a minute. I mean it, totally step back and take a good, hard look at what you're doing. Leaving your whole country behind, your family, your job…? For a man you've known less than a —"

"First of all," Jess cut in bitterly, "I never once said anything about leaving my job."

"Okay."

"Secondly, you know as well as I do that the only family I've got left is my mother."

Evie sucked in a breath, her expression pained.

"Besides you, Evie. You know what I meant. Thirdly," Jess continued. "Fernando and I have known each other more than six months. Maybe not in a way that you think is important, but it certainly meant something to me. The truth is, I've known Fernando for a long time, but the side of him I saw was different. That different side wasn't unattractive either, Evie. He's a seriously capable business man, incredibly intelligent, and maddeningly quick with the quip. Facts are, if he hadn't suggested running away to La Esperanza del Corazón, I might have recommended running off to Pamplona myself."

"Come on."

"I mean it."

"You're becoming incredibly defensive for one reason and one reason only."

Jess set her hand on her hip. "Oh? Why's that?"

"Because you know I'm right."

Jess inhaled a deep breath, then let it out slowly.

"Generally, you're right, Evie. I'll definitely give you that. But, this time, you're dead wrong."

"Great. Then prove it."

Jess stared at her and shook her head.

"Jess, you've got to believe me. There's nothing in the world I want more than your happiness. Your *true* happiness. Because I love you," she said, her voice lightly cracking.

Jess felt a pang of uneasiness. She completely loved Evie too. Always had, forever would. Nobody else had stuck by her the way Evie had. And, she knew in her soul, would continue to. "I love you too," she said, meaning it absolutely and hugging her tightly. But she also adored Fernando and needed to stay with him. The fates had placed him in her path for a reason. The two of them just weren't well suited—they were destined. Weren't they?

"But, Evie, you don't know what it's like when I'm with him. When Fernando and I are together, it's like that's where I'm meant to be—where I should stay."

"Exactly why I'm asking you to step away."

Jess withdrew, breaking Evie's embrace.

"Look," Evie said with sincere chestnut-brown eyes. "I'm not one to argue with destiny, but I also know that making the right decision, a careful one, takes time. What's so wrong with going back to America and thinking things over? Go back to work, check in with your mom, go out for a bagel in Brooklyn…"

"And then?"

"Jess, if your heart tells you it's right, you'll know. Then you can move forward. No second thoughts. Without regrets."

Jess's heart sank because she knew Evie was right. As much as she believed herself to have fallen in love with Fernando, maybe she needed some distance between them so she could assure herself her feelings were real. She'd be taking a risk, and she knew it. If she walked away now, she stood the chance that Fernando might tell her to never come back. But if he loved her as much as he said, wouldn't he do her that one small courtesy and wait?

"How long, Jessica?" Fernando asked. "How long are you asking me to do this? Two weeks? Three months? A year?" He stood in the room of their lovely hotel, his face wrought with pain.

Jess wrung her hands together, her stomach clenched. "I don't know," she answered honestly. If she said two weeks, what if she needed one week more? It didn't seem right for him to place her under a strict deadline.

"So it could be as much as a year?"

He studied her with disappointment, his disapproval agonizing. "Beautiful, Jessica. Just perfect. You're willing to make me wait past my thirty-second birthday."

"I thought you loved me."

"And I thought the feeling was mutual," he said, a cold burn in his green gaze. "Forgive me for being a fool."

Fernando turned away and began shoving clothes in his backpack.

Fear sliced through her at the thought that she was pushing him away. "It doesn't have to be like this."

"Like what?" he asked, scorching her with his glare. "Like you're asking me to risk everything? Lose my inheritance—the ranch—on the off chance you might come around?"

Jess's cheeks flamed as she spoke past the tightness in her throat. "I never said it was an *off chance*."

"No?" he asked combatively. "Then give me some odds, why don't you? Fifty percent? Seventy-five?"

"Please," she moaned, tears now streaming down her cheeks. "Fernando, stop!"

He blew a hard breath, then gathered himself, nabbing his wallet off the nightstand.

"Where are you going?" she asked, her head and heart crazed with emotion. She was leaving, and he was about to tell her to never return.

"To settle our bill," he said, halfway to the door.

When he stepped into the hall, she called after him, her voice trembling. "I thought it wasn't about the money."

He stopped in his tracks and stared her down. "Honestly," he said, "I don't know what it was about."

He pulled the door shut with a bang that sent her heart racing and the tears more furiously flowing down her face.

She'd lost him now.

It was done.

Fernando watched Jessica climb into the cab where Eve was waiting, the shadows from Casa Garcia de la Vega looming large ahead. If he wanted an easy way out, he could blame the best friend. But Fernando knew in his heart that had Jessica truly wanted to stay, no amount of congenial history could have convinced her otherwise. Gustavo appeared at his side, Fernando's best stallion at the ready.

"You can always go after her," Gustavo said.

"I already did," Fernando replied, stone-faced. He mounted his horse as the taxi started down the drive, Eve turning slightly to give him a guilty glance over her shoulder.

"Yah!" he commanded, driving his steed forward and alongside the road that carried Jessica's cab toward the airport. She pursed her lips and peered at him through the glass as he galloped faster. *Stop the car*, he wanted her to say. Anything to indicate they still stood a chance.

He followed them past the grove of olive trees, then slowed his horse in the setting sun.

Jessica turned away, her head dropping on Eve's shoulder.

Fernando swallowed past the burn in his throat and beat back the fire in his eyes.

Then he urged his horse into a run and took off over the desert landscape. He would ride until neither he nor his steed could take any more. But Fernando knew he would never outrace the ache in his soul. It was a scar he'd be forced to wear, just like the one on his thigh. Some battles were worth fighting, and Fernando had never found a contest in which he hadn't given it his all. Yet sometimes your opponent was tougher than you were, and—no matter how many skirmishes you won—you still wound up losing the war.

Fernando rode faster, leaning into the Andalusian winds. Tomorrow was his thirty-first birthday, but apparently, nobody remembered but him.

Eve pulled a tissue from her purse and handed it to Jess, who was weeping on her shoulder. It was one of those quiet sort of cries, tears spilling silently as Jess gazed straight ahead with unseeing eyes. Eve felt all punched out inside, as if a million tiny fists were beating at her gut and heart. She'd done the right thing, she was sure of it. What sort of friend might she have been had she left Jess here all alone to fend for herself with a man who looked like *him*?

Eve watched as Fernando quickened the pace of his horse and rode off into the sunset. If he'd really been sincere and not just trying to secure an inheritance, Jess's timeline wouldn't have mattered to him in the least. But he'd been unable to wait for her, had refused her point-blank. It was a miracle they'd gotten to the magistrate in time.

Eve glanced at the thick express mail package still clutched in Jess's hands. She'd held it on her lap since leaving Casa de la Vega, just gripping it there like some sort of lifeline between the reality of now and the hopeful imaginings of the past. Initially, the postmaster at the magistrate's office had been unhelpful, stating if the package had come through at the start of the week, it had likely been processed and was already on its way to Madrid for final approval. It was only at Eve's insistence that he'd dug through the large canvas carrier on stout wheels and managed to come up with the return address of La Esperanza del Corazón. The postmaster had required identification but then wasn't sure who to hand the package to. *"Give it to her,"* Fernando had said coldly. *"There's nothing left in it for me."*

When Jess had refused to take it, Eve had snatched it away, holding on to it until just now. Jess had accepted the parcel without a word and had just stared out the window at Fernando instead. Eve knew she must be disappointed to have met yet another man who wouldn't stand by her, but best to learn that now than a continent's move away and a few kids into the future.

"I booked us a long layover in Madrid," she said to Jess. "Fourteen hours. Plenty of time to clear out your apartment and spend a quick night."

Jess nodded numbly, staring down at the package. "I can't even remember what I left at that place."

"Probably not too much important," Eve answered. "But it's good to check it out, just in case. Jess?" Eve said, giving her shoulder a tight hug. "Please say you don't hate me?"

Jess stared at her, stunned. "Oh, Evie," she said with moist eyes. "I don't hate you. Don't hate you at all. I understand what you did and why you felt you had to do it. You didn't come all the way over here for yourself. You did it for me."

Eve's heart felt a little lighter. Maybe things would eventually get back to normal after all. Jess would put Fernando behind her and resume her life in Brooklyn. As time passed, she might even look back on this episode with the matador and thank Eve for coming to her rescue in Spain.

"It's only that…" Jess continued, her voice trailing off into melancholy.

"What is it, Jess? What?"

Jess set her chin a moment, focusing hard on something internal. When she turned to Eve again, her expression was drawn. "It's only that I wonder if maybe I'm"—her lips trembled—"starting to hate myself."

"Oh, Jess, no. Don't say that." Eve drew Jess into her arms as the airport tower loomed near. "Don't ever say that. Nobody could ever do anything but love you."

But by the way Jess crumbled in her embrace, it didn't appear she believed it.

"Fernando," Ana María said. "Do you mind telling your mother what's going on?"

Fernando had just come in from a long ride and didn't appear to be in the mood for talking.

"I'll tell you later," he said, heading for the study.

Ana María held out a hand to stop him. "You'll tell me now."

He turned on her, his expression surly.

Ana María pressed on, undaunted. "Your wife of one week gets in a cab bound for New York? I deserve to know."

His eyes were dark and stormy, like the sky before hard rain. "I need some time, Mamá."

"Fernando," she said, raising her voice for emphasis. "She's carrying your child, my grandbaby."

He met her with a hard, even stare. "There is no baby."

Ana María cupped her hand to her lips.

"Never was," he continued, his neck coloring. "I'm sorry that I lied to you."

Ana María stood there, dumbfounded. Fernando was stubborn, yes. Perhaps a little too used to getting his way. But never in his life had he lied to her. It took her a long while to form the words. "Why did you?" she asked quietly.

Fernando ran a hand through his hair, appearing at a loss, then hung his head for a prolonged beat. He slowly raised his eyes to hers. "Because, Mamá, in a crazy sort of way, I wanted it all to be real. Me, Jessica, our future together, a family…" He shrugged and gave a halfhearted smile that wrenched her through and through. "I let my emotions get the better of me. And that's something you taught me never to do."

Ana María reigned in her burgeoning tears, her heart breaking for her son. This wasn't about his birthday or the inheritance or their ranch. Fernando had finally fallen for a woman, and she'd simply slipped away. "You must fight for her," Ana María said.

Fernando shook his head. "I fought as hard as I know how." As he turned and walked away, Ana María heard him speak bitterly over his shoulder. "I can't convince a woman to love me who doesn't. In fact, I wouldn't even want to try."

Chapter Twelve

Jessica lifted the manila file folder from the small business desk in the Madrid apartment. "It's a good thing we stopped by here. I'd forgotten all about this."

Eve shot her a quizzical look.

"It's the contract, Evie. The acquisitions deal. It's what I flew to Madrid for."

"Then the whole trip wasn't a loss," Evie tried to add brightly.

"Right," Jessica said, setting the file folder back down and sounding less than convinced. Jess turned and walked to the french doors opening onto a small balcony. "I don't really blame him, you know. Fernando."

"Well, you certainly can't blame yourself." Jess glanced at her.

"Or me!" Eve rushed to say. She thumbed her chest, squeaking weakly. "Really, Jess. Tell me you're not blaming me?"

"I'm old enough to make up my own mind," she said, stepping outdoors.

But was she really? Just think of the mess she'd made of things in less than eight days! Evie nabbed a pencil off the desk and twisted up her hair. Somebody had to be the grown-up here, and since it hadn't been Jess, Eve had been forced to take the role. Surely, Jess would see that, once the dust settled and the emotional haze surrounding her cleared.

Jess seemed to be leaning over the balcony railing, teetering toward the street below. She couldn't possibly be despondent enough to toss herself over the edge. "Jess, don't!" Eve cried, rushing forward and lunging for her waist.

Jessica lost hold of the watering can she'd been gripping, and it clattered to the street. "Don't what?" she asked with dismay. "Water the flowers? Good God, Evie. Someone could have been walking by down below."

Evie stared into the small window box weeping with bright, harmonious colors, and practically wanted to cry herself. "I'm sorry," she said, catching her breath. "I thought—"

Jess set her hand on her hip and cocked her head sideways. "That what? I was going to jump?" Her blue gaze looked clear and reasonable, suddenly making Evie feel the fool and the youngest child in the place.

Eve's face burned hot as she ducked back inside. "You had to see it from my angle."

The realization hit Jess with a jolt. That was the issue, wasn't it? She'd always seen things from someone else's perspective. First, there was her mother who wanted her to go into banking. She was right, of course, because that was where the money was. And also, according to her mom, lots of single men. What her mother had failed to advise was that single didn't always equal decent and that sometimes even the decent ones didn't stick around.

Then there was Evie, forever filled with good advice, helping her think things out when life got too crazy.

"Jess? Are you all right?" Evie asked, peering at her from around the corner. First she thought Jess was a jumper, now she was homicidal?

"What are you doing hiding in there?"

"I just wanted to be sure that it's safe to come out and play."

Jess studied Evie with a long sigh. "I'm not tossing you over for a new best friend anytime soon."

Eve swallowed hard and nodded. "Good, that's very good to hear, you know."

"I would, however, probably like you a lot better if you could do me one favor."

"Anything, as long as you step away from that railing. Honestly, it looks kind of unsteady to me."

Jess stepped away from the wrought-iron grate and sat in an outdoor chair. "Why don't you grab that bottle of red wine and a couple of glasses," she said. "Then come back out here. There's something I'd like to talk through with you."

Two empty wineglasses sat on the table between them as the sky lightened with daybreak.

"I wish I could say we'd solved all the world's problems," Eve offered apologetically.

"There's no easy answer, is there?"

"Oh, Jess," Eve answered truthfully, "I don't think there are ever any easy answers."

"But Evie, can't you see? You've always told me what to do."

"Not this time," Eve said, crossing her arms firmly over her chest.

"What do you mean?"

"Jess, this isn't some casual hookup you're considering. You're talking a decision that affects the rest of your life. Who better to make that than you?"

"But you came all the way over here to stop me."

"No. I came all the way over here to see if you were still you. Someone had radically changed up my best friend, and it scared me silly."

"That someone being Fernando."

"Actually, I think that someone was you."

"Me?"

Evie studied her sincerely. "Look, I've known you a long time. What's it been?"

"Fifteen years."

"There you have it. That's longer than some marriages last!"

"So?"

"So, I've come to know you pretty well." Evie studied Jess and thoughtfully stroked her chin. "Maybe I didn't believe it in New York, but maybe that's because I had to see it with my own eyes. I don't know what precisely happened between you and Fernando, but it was obviously something that affected you both. Affected you, deeply. Christ! We wouldn't have pulled an all-nighter on this balcony if that wasn't the case. So now here you are, once again spilling your soul to me and asking me to put things right. Jess, I love you dearly. But, frankly, that's way too much responsibility. I can't even manage my hair most days."

Proving her point, she pulled the pencil from her hair, letting it spill in an unruly mass to her shoulders. They shared companionable laughter, after which Jess stated seriously, "Oh, Evie, what would I do without you?"

"Live your life," she answered. "A real grown-up life."

Jess picked up the empty wine bottle and traced its label, one very memorable vintage coming to mind. First, it was her mother, telling her what to do. Next, it was Evie, but mostly because Jess asked for it. Then there was Fernando, begging her to remain his bride. Had Jess wanted to stay merely because he'd asked her or because that was what she'd truly wanted to do?

"A life where I make my own choices, you mean."

"Who better to make them than you?" Evie asked.

"I don't think it's fair to ask me to pick which present to open first, Mamá. I wouldn't want to appear to play favorites."

"But Fernando," Ana María said lightly. "All of the gifts are from me."

"Not all of them," Gustavo said, stepping onto the patio. Consuelo trailed him, carting a lovely homemade flan.

Fernando grinned at the older woman. "Why, Consuelo, you've outdone yourself—again."

She giggled gratefully. "You're favorite, señor, with hints of toasted almond."

"I have something for you too," Gustavo said, as he pulled a wrapped bundle from behind his back.

"You don't mind?" Fernando asked his mother.

"No, please..." she encouraged merrily.

Fernando smiled, digging into the package.

"Oh my..." he said, opening the broad folds of an elegant matador's cape. "It's terrific."

"Where did you get it?" Ana María asked, her face registering mild shock.

"At the Plaza de Toros gift shop in Seville. It's not quite as fine as the one your father used, but it's a close replica."

Fernando stood to hug him soundly. "Thank you, Gustavo. I'll have to take this out and give it a whirl."

"Not in the true sense, I hope," Ana María said with a worried frown.

"I think that's it," Jess said, latching her suitcase.

"Good," Eve said. "Our taxi will be here any minute."

Jess carefully perused the small luxury apartment, thinking there were many things she was going to miss about coming here. Easy access to the city park and just a short stroll to the Prado. Plus, the numerous restaurants and produce vendors.

"Madrid's been a good assignment," she told Eve as they stepped onto the sidewalk fanning the broad boulevard.

"The next one may be even better. Who knows? Maybe you'll get sent to Venice or something."

"I think I'll steer clear of Venice in the summer."

"Some people!" Evie teased. "You've just become a big jet-setter and already you're complaining about the perks."

But the main perk on Jess's mind stood about six feet tall and had gorgeous green eyes. She'd never imagined during her initially maddening interactions with the Spaniard that she'd wind up falling in love with him. Wait one minute. Hold the phone. Did she just think *love*?

"Ouch! Watch what you're doing?"

"Huh?"

"Earth to Jessica Bloom," Evie cried. "You just dropped your whopping suitcase on my foot!"

"Oh my gosh, Evie!" Jess said, pulling it off. "I don't know what I was thinking!"

But clearly she did. She was thinking, mighty hard, about the fact that her heart had just tumbled down about one hundred thousand green grass hills. Over and over again.

"Evie," she said, feeling her face flush. "What day is it?"

"June tenth. Why?"

Jess glanced at the boarding pass in her hand, then waved it manically in the air.

"June *tenth*? Are you serious?" she asked as the cab pulled up.

"As serious as a heart attack, unless you're about to have one for me. Which you look like you might do at any second."

Maybe her heart had stopped. It was kind of like getting hit upside the head, only being hit harder. The thing was, while it might have halted for a moment, it was beating briskly now. So rapidly she thought she'd faint from its overexertion. Jess didn't need her mother to tell her or Evie to advise her or even Fernando to cajole her into something she already wanted to do. All Jess had to do was listen to that not-so-quiet inner voice that practically screamed at her not to get into that cab.

The taxi driver reached for her bag, but she pulled it back.

Evie raised her brow. "He just wants to put it in the trunk for you."

"I know," Jess said quickly. "But I think I'll need it." And she was going to need a lot more. Her whole wardrobe, in fact. Plus, there were other things in Brooklyn. Perhaps Evie could send them, or maybe she and Fernando could fly back for the move. Move! Jess was moving to Spain!

She stared at Evie with urgency. "Do you still have that express mail package?"

"You've got it. In the large duffle. Remember?"

Yes, it was all coming back in a whirl. She'd kept it completely intact, not bearing to break its seal. "Oh, right."

Jess unzipped her carry-on, telling the cabbie they'd just be a minute. "Here," she said, shoving the merger paperwork at Evie. "Do be a dear and drop this off at my office."

"You're not coming with me?" Evie asked, stunned.

"I can't. I'm still married...in the eyes of the church."

Fernando crossed himself devoutly, then stood from where he'd knelt before his father's portrait in the study. He was fully dressed for battle for the first time in a decade, and he thrilled at the rapidity of his pulse coursing through his veins. To an outsider, this walk down memory lane may have seemed frivolous, but to Fernando it was deadly important.

He had failed—and failed badly—at the first real thing in his life, capturing the heart of the lady he loved. That had made him feel more than inadequate; in many ways, it had left him believing he was less than a man. The cape had been the perfect gift. Gustavo knew him so well. While Fernando didn't intend to return to the corrida, he still needed to prove something to himself. He needed to climb back in the ring and face the beast, most especially the raging animal that scraped about angrily inside of him.

Fernando had left bullfighting for the love of a woman and now was forced to return for similar reasons. While he'd forgone uncertain dangers in deference to his mother, he needed to confront them now out of respect for himself. If he didn't, Jessica's memory would crush him for eternity. Fernando needed to prove himself stronger than that.

Fernando scooped up the cape and held it in his broad hand, slicing it expertly through the air.

"Going out?" Gustavo asked, appearing in the doorway.

"I thought I would."

"Then, I'll come and serve as your second."

A matador always needed a watchman, especially in practice sessions as precarious as this one, where there were no medical personnel on site and the nearest hospital was more than ninety kilometers away.

"You're a good friend, Gustavo," Fernando said.

"Your mother would disagree. She's very put out with me for planting the idea in your head."

"You may have planted, amigo. But, the seeds had already been sown. I would have been driven to this, regardless."

Gustavo didn't argue because he knew it was true. He stared down at Fernando's empty hand. "Where's your sword?"

"This is a test of skill today, nothing more," he said, patting his friend on the shoulder. "I'm not in it for the kill."

"You might not be," Gustavo answered. "But what about him?"

"They've gone, señora," Consuelo said. "You asked me to advise you."

Ana María sat staring straight ahead and sipping her sherry. She was on a bench in her rose garden, one of the places she loved best. "Did Gustavo tell you which bull?"

"I'm not quite sure." But by the way Consuelo averted her eyes, Ana María guessed that she knew. It was Alejandro, the most dangerous beast in the lot. They couldn't even let him around the horses. The ranch hands all rumored Alejandro to be a little crazy. At one time, he'd been primed for the ring before being deemed too unpredictable. Ana María knew she should have sold Alejandro off long ago but had never quite had the heart. He would be put down immediately anywhere else. At least here he had some sort of life, as long as they kept him fairly well segregated.

"Shall I serve a late dinner?" Consuelo asked.

"No. Make it on time. I'm certain Fernando won't be gone long."

But, deep in her heart, Ana María feared she was losing him forever. Perhaps it was an irrational fear or—worse yet—a mother's intuition. She hadn't dared to see Fernando off, afraid of inviting bad luck. Best to sit here and enjoy her garden, thinking only of happy things on this sunny afternoon.

"As you wish," Consuelo said, taking her leave.

"Consuelo?" Ana María said, stopping her. "What did you think of the girl?"

Consuelo pursed her lips in thought. "She was very beautiful."

"I meant, what did you think of her for Fernando?"

"It's not my place, Doña Ana María."

"It is if I'm asking you."

Consuelo perused her frankly. "In that case, I thought she was good for Fernando. And that he was good for her. They were two very strong people, even stronger together, it seemed."

"Thank you, Consuelo. I value your opinion."

"It's sad it no longer matters."

"I'm sorry for Fernando that she's gone too. He's taken this really hard. But he'll bounce back. He's a de la Vega after all," she said with a reserved smile.

Chapter Thirteen

Jess couldn't have been any more excited had it been her own birthday. The moment she'd made the connection between Fernando and today's date, she'd viewed it as more than just a sign. Her leaving Iberia the day her new husband turned thirty-one clearly wasn't the way to behave. Apart from their elopement and glorious wedding night, it was the first true celebration the two of them would get to share. Jess had many gifts in store for Fernando, not the least of which she hoped to deliver in bed.

Her face heated at the memory of Fernando's flesh pressed to hers. There was a matrimonial union she could get used to, and not just because Fernando was the most skilled lover she'd ever had. He was also funny and kind, thought the world of his family, and had promised utter devotion to her. Surely it hadn't been long enough since he'd sincerely said his vows that Fernando had changed his mind.

"Casa Garcia de la Vega," she told the driver as she climbed into the cab at the small satellite airport. "And hurry, please."

Jess's heart raced at the thought of seeing him. Would he reject her at once, still scorned from her earlier rebuke, or accept her with open arms, sweeping her off her feet and carrying her up to his bed? No, he probably wouldn't do that straightaway, Jess realized. His mother most likely had a party planned. There'd be gifts to open and cake. And, if Consuelo had any say in it, a lavish birthday dinner besides. Jess checked her cell for the time as the sun sank low.

It was a special smart phone Fernando had given her in Seville during their first night there. Since her other hadn't worked in La Esperanza del Corazón, he'd presented her with this high-tech replacement that received service in any locale, even in the most remote regions of Africa. He'd programmed in just one number, his, and had promised to transfer her address book over once they'd returned to the ranch. But with Evie's unexpected arrival and Jess's rushed departure from town, the data transfer had never taken place.

Jess's thumb hovered over the single entry in her address book. Maybe she should call him now to say she was on the way. That would be the polite thing to do, wouldn't it? Give him a bit of warning. Jess considered her alternatives, weighing the fact that if she caught Fernando in an off mood, he just might get on his horse and decide to go on an eternal ride. If he was angry still and there was going to be some sort of showdown, best to have it occur first thing. Get it done with, so their *happily ever after* could begin. And it would start too. That was, if Jess had anything to do with it, which she most certainly intended to.

Jess surveyed the landscape of flowing sunflower fields and twisted almond groves, grasping the fact that this was her new home. It was a place she would grow to love, because it was a place she had selected. All her life, Jess had been told what to do, advised on the course which suited her best. Now, she had decided for herself to take this brave, untraveled path—and see where it led. She was over the moon at the thought of sharing it with Fernando, the sexy Spaniard who'd vowed to love and protect her, and to whom she wished to give her heart.

What this meant for her job, she wasn't sure, but she trusted Fernando would be supportive as she worked things out. Perhaps she could make an arrangement with her existing company, or maybe she'd be adventuresome and branch out, starting a new endeavor of her own. Whatever she would do, Jess would ensure the career choice was *hers*. Something that called to her and to which she could contribute. Something that made her proud of her efforts and tired with satisfaction at the end of each day.

They came to the turn in the drive to Casa Garcia de la Vega, which loomed large in its splendor before them. Jess realized with a smile that for most of her life she'd been running away. Suddenly, here she was in Spain, galloping ahead. If she could move any faster, she would. Oh, to see Fernando and tell him all that was in her heart and head. Jess was bursting with the moment as she leapt from the cab, nearly forgetting to pay the driver. He thanked her with a tip of his cap and left her standing on the large stone steps with her luggage.

Before this day ended, Jess's new life would begin.

Fernando stood in the ring, facing off, eye to eye, with Alejandro. The animal stood five feet at the shoulder, a mixture of muscle and menace. Fernando had never really known what had provoked Alejandro's ire, but he'd been ornery since the day he was born. When he'd been rejected as a candidate for the corrida, Ana María had next thought to place him in Pamplona. But the officials there investigated Alejandro's unsavory history with horses and had deemed him a bad risk for marauding tourists hoping to best the bulls during the July street fest. So he'd stayed on the ranch, his temperament worsening with age. He was now in the prime of his life, fiercely fit and unruly. Fernando lowered his cape as the beast scraped the dirt with his hoof. Then with a swish, he twirled the cape sideways as Alejandro tore by, barely breezing past Fernando's right side. Fernando turned on his heels, once more beckoning the bull. Each *paso* was perfect, his feet keeping rhythm with his body and expertly marking the tempo of the fluttering red cape.

A noise erupted in Fernando's ears, the sweet cacophony of the crowd urging him on. "*¡Olé!*" Fernando shouted as Alejandro passed him by yet again, this time on his left. Theirs was an intricate dance, a ballet, really, and Fernando delighted in his practiced control—each muscle primed and ready. This was the life he was born to. He loved the corrida and couldn't deny it. Every ounce of his soul keened in the wind as he scarcely missed the deadly horns. Fernando buckled as Alejandro swept by once more, skillfully avoiding danger. He'd been gored once and didn't long to repeat it. His whole life had flashed in one instant at the tender age of twenty-three. He saw Gustavo sitting on the fence, strong arms steadying his position on the railing. It had been Gustavo, nine years ago, who'd pulled him from near-certain death. *¡Olé!*

Fernando felt his sweat building, steaming his temples. *¡Olé!*

While he was not as young as he'd once been, he still had the stamina of teenagers half his age. Hadn't he proved that time and again with Jessica? In thinking of her, he spied a heavenly image. The love of his life racing toward him. *No, a mirage.* Had to be. So then why did she smile sweetly and call out his name? And Gustavo, rushing to her, begging her to quell her eager cries…

Fernando turned toward the bull, seconds too late, to find Alejandro nearly upon him. Jessica's eyes flashed with terror as Gustavo lunged forward.

"Fernando!" she called in a voice shrill with panic. The thud-thud, thud-thud, thud-thud of menacing hoofbeats thundered near. Alejandro lowered his head, positioned for a death thrust. He was angry and tired of these human creatures that continued to torment him.

Jess stopped short, caught in Gustavo's quick embrace. "Leave it," he said, his tone terse.

But how could she leave what she witnessed happening before her? Fernando was about to get gored by a bull, most certainly on account of her! She'd distracted him at a critical moment, leaving him limited time to react. *Oh my God, not now!* Not her dear Fernando. Tears burned hot down Jess's checks as Fernando turned on the bull, confronting him head-on. What impressed Jess most was Fernando's calm. He didn't flinch. He didn't back away. Just stood there, poised and ready. Seconds ticked by like hours as the bull advanced.

And then, without warning, Fernando lunged forward, seizing the enormous beast by his horns. In a flash, Fernando flipped over him, landing hard with one shoulder to the animal's back and then crashing in a heap to the ground.

Gustavo released Jess and raced into the ring, swinging open its gate and coaxing the bull outside. He bolted back toward Fernando, panting, to find Jess hopelessly wailing at his side.

Chapter Fourteen

Jess sat in the beautifully designed living area, not daring to meet Señora Garcia de la Vega's eyes. She blamed Jess, of course. The accident never would have happened without Jess's unexpected arrival and invasion on the scene. Gustavo had assisted in getting Fernando upstairs, and the doctor had been with them for over an hour. Jess wanted to pray but wasn't sure it would count. She wasn't exactly in with the Holy Savior, and the one here went through the pope besides. Jess wouldn't know where to begin other than to suggest lighting candles. That sounded right and was something they always did in movies.

"Would it help if we lit some candles?" she lamely asked Fernando's mom.

Ana María's charcoal gaze fell on hers. "The electricity works just fine."

"Right," Jess said, pressing her knees together firmly. She'd worn a short dress, one she'd thought was sexy. The fashion change-up had been impromptu and had occurred once Evie had taken her leave. After Jess declared she wasn't going back to New York, Eve initially hadn't understood her reservation about sharing the taxi. "Well, you've got to get back to the airport, haven't you?" was all Evie had asked. The truth was, Jess did need to get to the airport. But first she had a few essential items to take care of, like stopping by the main post office and changing into an outfit that would sweep a matador off his feet.

Jess sucked in a breath, realizing she'd done more than that. She'd landed him facedown in the dirt. If Fernando were hurt in any substantial way, she'd never forgive herself, or her designer mini either. Fernando had always been fond of her legs. Perhaps their full revelation at such a critical moment had proved disastrous. No, Jess couldn't take full credit for that. It wasn't really her fault Fernando had gotten hurt, was it? And he couldn't be hurt in any horrible way if he'd been able to let Gustavo help him up the stairs.

The doctor appeared, traipsing down the steps, a limp stethoscope strung around his neck.

Ana María stood tensely.

"He wants to see you," the old man said, staring straight at Jess.

A wellspring of hope arose in her heart. "He's all right?" Jess asked.

"A little sore, but yes, he'll live."

"Thank God," Ana María said, sinking back in her chair.

Jess stood and straightened her skirt, hoping she still looked all right. It had been one hell of an afternoon, and she still had to ensure that she and Fernando would have one hell of a night.

"How bad are his injuries?" she tactfully asked the doctor.

"Probably best if you talk to him yourself," the doctor said.

Jess crept up the steps, unsure of what she might find. Would Fernando be furious at her for causing him pain or merely delusional from his bump on the head? At the very least, he had to have a mild concussion. Jess dug into her inner resources, pressing herself forward. She was a stronger person than she'd ever been. A person who now totally realized she loved and deserved Fernando. Just because she'd nearly gotten him killed that didn't mean they couldn't work past any differences. She hadn't done it on purpose, after all.

Jess paused a moment before the shut bedroom door. So many wonderful things had occurred in there and would many times again, if Fernando would only let Jess put her mind to it. She rapped lightly and waited a beat until Gustavo answered.

"Come in!" Gustavo called as she creaked the door open.

Gustavo stood from the chair where he'd sat at Fernando's bedside.

Fernando lay motionless in the big king-size bed. Given his typically olive complexion, he appeared much lighter to Jess --pallid even-- and she saw this as a dire sign. What if he was worse than the doc had let on? What if he wouldn't fully recover? "The doctor said—" she began.

"It's true," Gustavo agreed. "He wants to see you."

How that could be, considering he had his eyes tightly shut, Jess wasn't sure. Yet she clearly wasn't armed to argue. Maybe she could bring him back around. Yes, that's what Fernando needed. A little Florence Nightingaling.

"He's just resting," Gustavo assured her. "Why don't you sit with him awhile?"

Jess nodded and made her way to the bedside as Gustavo slipped from the room.

Silently, she took her seat, mentally kicking herself for every ounce of anguish she'd ever caused her loving husband. He was glorious and strong and brave...and...*argh*! Something reached out and grabbed for her hand. Reason dawned quickly telling her it was Fernando, appearing suddenly in the pink of health.

"*Querida*," he said, green eyes on hers. "You nearly killed me."

"Fernando!" she gasped, catching her breath. "You're okay."

He hadn't been on his deathbed at all. It was just Jess's guilty imagination that had caused her to think so.

"Some parts hurt more than others," he assured her.

Yes, and she felt terrible about that. More than terrible. "Is it your head?"

"Actually," he said, centering his gaze on hers, "it was my heart. Ironically, it seems to be feeling better."

"I'm glad," she offered sincerely.

Fernando stared at her, appearing more handsome than she'd ever known him, bare-chested beneath the covers.

"Why did you come back?" he asked.

Jess twisted her lips into a smile. "Because, you silly, there was a birthday party I couldn't miss."

"I'm afraid all the presents have been opened."

"Not all," she said with a wicked smile.

Fernando's mouth hung open. "Did my new wife lock the door?"

"She'd be glad to," Jess said, meaning it absolutely.

She couldn't wait to tell him about the package and the post office and her decision to live here forever. But for the next thirty minutes or so, maybe she would.

Fernando pulled her down on the bed, bringing her mouth to his.

"Are you're sure you're okay to do this?" she asked.

His body pressed forward in response. "What do you think?" he asked with a sexy grin.

"But what about your mother? Gustavo? The doctor?"

"I don't think any of them would blame me for recuperating," he said with a husky rasp.

Jess felt the heat sweep from her breasts to her deepest feminine regions. "You're not going to make me get naked now, are you?"

"I don't think we have time for that," he said, flipping her onto her back.

In a flurry of kisses, Fernando had pushed up her short skirt and pulled down her panties.

"Tell me that you want me to take you," he said, his tone urgent with desire.

"I want you to more than take me," Jess said, melting away.

Fernando raised his brow as he swept back blonde strands from her cheek.

"I want you to take me and keep me. Take me and keep me. Forever, please."

A broad, willing grin swept across Fernando's face.

"Anything—and everything—to keep my new wife happy."

Chapter Fifteen

Jess snuggled down under the covers, happily embraced in Fernando's arms.

"For a man just bested by a bull, you do all right," she said with a naughty grin.

He gently stroked her arm. "I only had the wind knocked out of me. A few bumps and bruises, but I'm fine."

"Lucky for us both." Jess kissed him sweetly.

"Yes," he said, squeezing her rump.

"Fernando." She raised her brow. "How did you do that thing with the horns?"

"It's an old trick my father taught me." He grinned, and the adoration in his eyes warmed her through and through. "A self-preservation technique."

"So you practiced it before?"

"My father threw me in the ring when I was five," he answered. "I didn't get to carry a weapon until I was twelve."

Jess cupped a hand to her mouth in horror. "You're kidding?"

"Nope."

Jess had heard of parents tossing their toddlers in a pool to teach them how to swim, but this seemed even worse. Truth was, neither scenario sounded very civilized to Jess. Surely Fernando wouldn't think to continue the barbaric tradition.

"Fernando…" she began with a tentative blush. "You wouldn't actually. What I mean is, not with our child…"

He tenderly massaged her belly through the sheet. "What was that you were saying about our baby, my wife?" he asked, giving her neck a sexy nibble.

"That's another thing I need to discuss with you."

Fernando tugged at the sheet, not dissuaded from his mission. "Boy... Girl... It doesn't matter. I will absolutely adore them both."

"Not that," she said, gripping the duvet and yanking it up from where it had nestled at their feet.

Fernando twisted his lips and eyed her curiously. "Cold, *querida*?"

"No, no." Jess's face caught fire. "All the opposite. Thank you."

"Then, what?"

"It's about our marriage. The papers..."

"We'll get all that straightened out as soon as you're ready."

Jess swallowed hard, gathering her courage. She hoped she'd done the right thing, making such an enormous unilateral decision. "I was ready about six hours ago."

"I'm sorry?" he asked, perplexed.

"The package, Fernando. When I was in Madrid, I took it to the central post office and mailed it." She ducked her head under the covers, not sure what sort of fireworks to expect. Her answer came in an explosion of laughter, a rich, rumbling tone that washed over her as Fernando gently peeled the covers away.

"Is that a fact?" he asked, green eyes merry.

She nodded silently.

Fernando cupped her chin in his hand, surveying her with loving eyes. "That's got to be the best birthday present I've ever gotten."

Ana María impatiently checked her watch.

"What is taking them so long up there? Maybe I should go and see."

Gustavo shot to his feet. "No, Doña Ana María. I'll go."

She took another sip of her sherry, scrutinizing. While Ana María rarely had a second glass, it was late in the afternoon, and she'd had a long day. The doctor had left with assurance Fernando would be back on his feet in no time. Only a scare, he'd said. Ana María frowned, thinking it was more like a brush with death.

Gustavo took his time on the stairs, dawdling, it seemed.

"Have you lost your way?" she asked him.

"No, señora," he said, waving his cell in her direction. "Just checking my texts."

"Well, for heaven's sake, do that later," she said, annoyed.

Gustavo quickened his pace, briskly moving up the stairs. Ana María didn't care what sort of apology Jessica was administering; it was long past the time it should have been over. Ana María widened her eyes, hoping Fernando and she hadn't been... But, of course, if she knew her son... Ana María sighed, supposing she should feel relieved he really was all right in that case.

As further proof, Fernando and Jessica paraded down the stairs, linked arm in arm. Gustavo trailed them.

"Feeling better?" Ana María asked, sternly raising an eyebrow.

"Yes, much!" Fernando proclaimed brightly. "Mamá," he said with a winning smile. "Jessica and I have the most amazing news."

Ana María listened to their story with the composure she'd taught herself to maintain under even the most trying circumstances. She wasn't that old of a woman, but still, this episode had taken her to task. First, Fernando was married; then Jessica was pregnant. Next, neither of them was either. Suddenly, again they were together, but her son had nearly died in the process. Ana María sighed heavily, praying the drama was over.

Jessica's cheeks went dusty rose as she turned beseeching blue eyes on Ana María.

"I know it started out kind of messy, Señora Garcia de la Vega. But the truth is, I really do love your son. I really hope you believe it, and that one day soon…maybe not right away…but over time…you'll come to accept me into your family.

Ana María flagged a palm in her direction. Fernando studied his mother with concern, protectively wrapping an arm around his bride.

"First," she said sternly, "I think we should dispense with that Señora Garcia de la Vega business. After all," she said, rising, "someday, in the not-too-distant future, I hope, you'll make me a grandmother."

Her lips drew into a smile as she welcomed her children with arms extended.

"Jessica. Fernando," she told them, hugging them together tightly. "My blessings on your union."

They hugged her back, Jessica unexpectedly releasing a few tears.

While Gustavo went for Consuelo and the champagne, Ana María took Jessica's hand in hers. "You can't possibly be married without a ring, my dear."

"I was planning to take care of it," Fernando rushed in. "I would have done so sooner if I'd known she was coming back."

"I'm sorry I didn't give you any warning," Jessica offered sincerely.

"No apologies necessary," Fernando said. "I'm just glad that you're here."

"That's makes all of us," Ana María said with a warm smile. She turned toward her son. "Now Fernando," she said, "about that ring…"

Fernando approached Jess on the patio, where she sat drinking her morning *café con leche.* He was devilishly handsome in his crisply pressed chinos and deep red polo, lending him that sexy matador edge. How Jess had ever second-guessed her gut instinct to marry him, she'd never know. She certainly wasn't doubting him now.

"Good morning, darling," he said, strolling over and stunning her with a whopping kiss.

"*Buenos días*," she replied, dabbing her moist lips with a napkin. He'd nearly scorched her with his lips. Not that she minded.

"Ah, Jessica," he said, taking her hands in his. "You look especially bride-like this morning."

Jess laughed, looking down, realizing she'd once more worn white. Naturally, it was summertime, but she couldn't help but think there was something subliminal to her dressing that way all the time.

"I own other color clothes, you know," she said with a smug little pout.

"And I'll get you some more," he assured her. "As many as you'd like. Though, in truth, I don't think a lot of clothing is necessary. Not given our plans for the immediate future."

"Plans?"

"I know you've always wanted to see Paris, but it's murder to visit the city in June. Too much heat, so many tourists. April is better. We can plan for next year."

"Fernando," she teased him lightly. "Just what are you getting at?"

His eyes twinkled with delight. "How does Fiji sound? A private honeymoon hut on the water, overlooking the fish through a window in the floor?"

Jess nearly spilled her coffee setting it down. "Really?" she asked with delight.

"You will need a bathing suit, of course."

Jess smiled up at him, thinking she'd honeymoon anywhere with this man. Even right here in La Esperanza del Corazón.

"But first," he said, surprising her by kneeling before her, "I think we should have a proper wedding, don't you?"

The truth was, she'd thought of nothing else since the moment she'd posted that package. Jess was bursting with joy and wanted the people she loved to share in it. Her mother and Evie…

"It doesn't have to be a big ceremony," she said, feeling the moisture in her eyes.

"Well, at least tell me I can invite Brother Emilio."

"How about Tía Margarita?"

He grinned, pulling a gorgeous antique ring from his pocket, an enormous diamond offset by rubies all around.

"Oh, Fernando," Jess gasped as tears sprang from her eyes. "It's beautiful."

"It belonged to my grandmother, given to her by my Grandfather Garcia de la Vega, the greatest bullfighter of the twentieth century." He shot her a sly wink. "Rubies are the sign of a matador, you know."

Fernando slowly slid the ring on her finger, finding it a little loose. He gave a worried frown. "We can get it sized."

"It's perfect," she said, her voice coming out as a whisper.

"We'll make it more perfect," he said with a smile.

Fernando gazed at her, and Jess saw tumbling summer hills, but this time she didn't mind free-falling. It was delightful and heady and fun. The best part was they were doing it together.

"I know I asked this before," he said, "but we were both a little...you know..." He made a wavering motion with his hand.

"I knew what I was doing," she challenged.

"Maybe. But you know it a lot more clearly now. Mrs. Jessica Bloom Garcia de la Vega," he said, taking her hand. "Will you marry me again in the presence of our families and inviting all those we know to share in the joy of our love?"

"Oh, Fernando," she said, springing into his arms. "I'll marry you as many times as you'd like."

Epilogue

The upscale outdoor wedding was conducted on the sprawling Garcia de la Vega estate. A stylized trellis studded with lovely white roses from Ana María's garden arched over the altar, nestled within a special grove of olive trees. The two mothers got on fabulously, while Evie flirted outrageously with a very handsomely turned out Gustavo. Everyone delighted in the morning, which was bright and sunny, the sweeping azure sky not sporting a single cloud.

Jess kissed Fernando for half an eternity, deciding to save the rest for their second wedding night. Repeating yourself didn't seem so bad when one put this spin on it. Fernando pulled back, apparently having been tapped on the shoulder.

"You're supposed to save that part until after the pronouncement," Father Domingo said.

"I'm sorry, Father," Fernando said, not sounding like he meant it. "You've got to admit the circumstances are extenuating. We are already married."

"In the eyes of the church," Jess said with a sheepish smile.

"And in the eyes of the law."

Seated wedding guests turned and looked at each other.

"What do you mean?" Jess asked her loving husband.

Fernando grinned, first at Jess and then at Father Domingo.

"Confirmation arrived from Madrid this morning. In the form of our marriage license."

Jess gasped with happy surprise. "Really?"

Fernando hung his head, then devilishly raised his eyes. "Actually, it came a few days ago, but it seemed fitting to save the news as a wedding gift."

"Shall we get on with it?" Father Domingo asked.

"Yes, let's," Jess said, thinking she couldn't love Fernando any more than she did at this moment.

Father Domingo finished his benediction, then introduced Mr. and Mrs. Fernando Garcia de le Vega to the elated crowd as husband and wife. Applause and cheers rang out all around.

Evie stood at Jess's side, holding her bridal bouquet and beaming with delight. "So that's how you do it."

"How I do what?" Jess asked as she linked arms with Fernando and turned for the recessional.

Evie adjusted her train, then whispered slyly, "How you marry a matador." Her eyes traveled to Gustavo, extra handsome in his boutonniere. "Think there might be one here for me?"

"I don't think Gustavo's a bullfighter," Jess whispered back, accepting her flowers.

"I might have to check and see if he has a scar," Evie said a little too loudly.

Fernando playfully narrowed his eyes at his bride. "You haven't been talking, *querida*?"

Jess just pursed her lips until they burst into a smile. "Not in detail," she replied hastily. She may have bragged on him a bit, but a girl could hardly blame her. He was to die for, after all. And she hadn't said a thing to anyone but Evie.

"Good," he said, snuggling her affectionately against his side. "Some things are meant to be just between a husband and wife."

"Fernando," she said fondly, "there are many things just between us."

"As the years go by," he said, "I hope there will be many more."

"Actually," she said coquettishly, "there might be one more fairly soon."

Fernando's face lit up like the most brilliant Andalusian sunrise.

"Is that a fact?"

"Just promise me we'll work out a compromise on the bulls."

"*¡Olé!*" he said, sealing his pledge with a kiss.

Somewhere in the distance, champagne corks popped as Jess's heart soared to the moon. Tomorrow morning, they were going to Fiji. Afterwards, she'd offered to help Fernando revamp his business here. Garcia wines held a lot of promise. If they started exporting their product, that promise could double. Jess didn't know wines, but she knew international business. Plus, she'd have a willing partner to help her along. Fernando loved the idea of her becoming involved in the family business, and Ana María was thrilled Jess had taken an interest too. Jess's mom and Evie were invited to visit at any time. By the look in her best friend's eye, Jess thought with a smile, Evie's next trip to Iberia might be coming soon.

THE END

A Note from the Author

Thanks for reading *How to Marry a Matador*. I hope you enjoyed it. If you did, please help other people find this book.

1. This book is lendable, so loan it to a friend who you think might like it so that she (or he) can discover me too.

2. Help other people find this book: write a review.

3. Sign up for my newsletter so that that you can learn about the next book as soon as it's available. Write to GinnyBairdRomance@gmail.com with "newsletter" in the subject heading.

4. Visit my website for details on other books available now: http://www.GinnyBairdRomance.com.

Also By Ginny Baird

The Sometime Bride
Real Romance
Santa Fe Fortune
The Christmas Catch
The Holiday Bride

To see an excerpt from *Santa Fe Fortune,*
keep reading for a sneak peek here!

SANTA FE FORTUNE

"I had a really great time tonight," she said, beaming up at him and feeling very much as if it had been a date.

"Me too," he said, stepping a fraction of an inch closer. Sea-blue eyes washed over her, threatening to pull her under. And boy, did she want to get swept away. "I'm glad you agreed to see me tomorrow, even if it's just an arrangement."

Gwen sensed Dan could rearrange her heart every which way, if she wasn't careful. "I'm glad I'm seeing you too," she said, feeling the warmth in her cheeks.

"Ten o'clock work for you?" he asked, his tone growing gravelly.

"Uh-huh," she uttered, mesmerized by his gaze.

He moved nearer now, his mouth just inches away. "I'll be damned if I don't want to kiss you," he said, his voice a husky rasp.

And she'd be damned if she didn't want him to. "Dan..." she said, tilting up her chin and closing her eyes.

"But I won't," he said, snapping her back to attention, eyes open. "Not now. Not here. Not like this..."

She started to speak as he brought his fingers to her lips. "If ever I've seen a woman who deserves to be kissed well, it's you. But the timing has got to be right. You have to be sure." He cast a cursory glance at her wedding band and backed away. "I need to be sure. Something tells me we've both gone down a path neither of us wants to travel again..."

Chapter One

Gwendolyn Marsh leaned across the large oak table that served as a desk. "I'm going to be honest with you, Mr. Holbrook. I didn't fly all the way out here to get swindled."

Dan stared in disbelief at the incredibly contentious woman. *Swindled* was an awfully big accusation coming from such a small frame. She couldn't stand more than five foot five in heels, and she'd nearly tumbled off them striding into the place.

"Like I told you, Mrs. Marsh, I'm not in the position to make that decision. If two thousand a canvas is what Ms. Holstein quoted you in the email, then I'm afraid I'll need to stick by that."

Soft gold curls fell at uneven angles, framing a lovely face as deep brown eyes homed in on him. If she weren't so hard-edged, he might consider her beautiful. Dan stopped himself, realizing appraisals of the clientele weren't in his job description.

"It's *Ms.,* if you must know."

Some lucky fellow was off the hook.

"My apologies. I saw the wedding band and…"

"It's a relic, okay? I haven't gotten used to going without it."

"I'm sorry, I had no idea. I understand it takes a while."

She leveled him a look, as if he were the culprit. Hey, maybe in her eyes, all men were. Dan had met the type before and could easily read the signs: *steer clear, not for you buddy, a sexy woman's not everything…* Sexy? Did he just think *sexy?* Gwendolyn Marsh wasn't movie-star thin like most females here. Her formfitting sundress hugged every curve in just the right way. Wrong way, as far as he was concerned. This was just another sign he'd been alone too long. It wasn't like Dan didn't have his reasons. In fact, when he was being honest, Dan realized he was likely worse news for her than she was for him. All women after a while had hopes, dreams…and Dan Holbrook was just the man to dash them.

Dark eyes sparked with fierce determination. "I think I'd like to speak to Ms. Holstein myself."

"I'm afraid that won't be possible."

She arched one perfectly manicured eyebrow. "Why not?"

This was just what Dan needed, a hot-tempered, hot-bodied woman waltzing into his Santa Fe gallery on a hot July afternoon. Okay, it wasn't technically his gallery…

Dan cursed himself for his soft spot in agreeing to run the place while Nancy was away. He didn't even like being indoors.

"Ms. Holstein is in the south of France, will be until next month."

She pulled her naturally plump lips into a thin pink line. "I see." She faltered slightly, nearly losing her composure. There was sheen to her eyes that made them look moist. Dan hoped she wasn't about to break down crying. Nancy had assured him this would be easy, just a few clients flying in from out of state. Surprise negotiations and weepy women weren't in the mix. Negotiations Dan could handle. Weepy women were another story.

A bell tinkled above the door, and a couple of well-dressed patrons entered, a man in an expensive suit and a woman wearing a tailored dress and high-end cowgirl boots.

"Be right with you folks," Dan told them, surmising these were the buyers from Los Angeles.

Gwen stood, apparently taking this as a dismissal. "Well, I guess that's it, then." She tucked her clutch under one arm and thrust forward the opposite hand. "Thanks for your time."

Dan sent a furtive glance at the Californians perusing shelves of New Mexican pottery and pretending not to listen. "Ms. Marsh, I'm afraid we got off on the wrong…" She tapped a strappy sandal, sporting bright painted nails and multiple toe rings. Heat rose at Dan's nape as his gaze eased up shapely legs. "…foot."

She withdrew her hand and cocked her head sideways, waiting.

"What I mean is, please sit back down, and let's discuss this like reasonable people. I'm sure we can work something out." Dan cringed at the sound of his own voice. Groveling? Here was a word not even in his vocabulary, yet he was being just about as placating as humanly possible. Dan wasn't doing it for himself, he remembered. He was doing this for Nancy. Other than the day-to-day oversight of things, which really was no problem, she'd given him only two jobs to do. Surely a man as capable at cutting deals as he was wouldn't have trouble selling a few items to some Los Angeles industry execs and buying canvases from an easy-going North Carolina native. Dan had a notion Nancy had never met Gwendolyn Marsh face-to-face when she'd made the latter assessment.

The hardness lining her eyes eased just a little. "I suppose I could stay for a bit," she said, her voice taking on the lilt of the mid-Atlantic South. She took her seat, splaying the lap of her flowered sundress across tightly nestled knees.

The Californians tastefully removed themselves to the back of the gallery to study a photographic desert landscape series, and Dan sat as well. He plucked a hanky from his suit pocket and dabbed the back of his neck, thinking it had to be over a hundred degrees in here.

Something tender welled in Dan's throat, and he realized he wasn't just doing this for Nancy. For some inexplicable reason, he felt driven to be nice to Ms. Marsh for her own sake. Never mind that she'd practically bulldozed right over him crashing in here. After all, he'd dealt with worse in business before. The truth was Nancy had given him some leeway. If Marsh really pushed, Dan could go up as high as three thousand a pop, mostly because Nancy had faith in Marsh's work and thought it was good. Nancy also believed that Marsh could develop a Santa Fe following. Many of the buyers here came from the West Coast, and Marsh's oils capturing snippets of sea life would be a ready sell. Dan had seen the slides, and they were impressive. Borrowing more from impressionism than realism, Marsh had a way of zeroing in on the smallest, seemingly inconsequential detail, like an isolated seashell, and illuminating it in a special and grandiose way.

She opened her purse and withdrew a thin ledger. "If you'd let me show you my figures, I'm sure you'll understand why my prices have gone up."

Dan scanned the haphazardly arranged numbers, deciding she was no mathematician. He pointed to one clumsily assumed total. "I can understand where material costs have climbed, but how exactly is it that your hourly rate has doubled?"

"Hard times, Mr. Holbrook," she said without flinching. "Don't you read the papers?"

"*Wall Street Journal* and you?" he bantered without skipping a beat.

"Well, I...read, of course." With that, she awkwardly angled an elbow and sent her clutch crashing to the floor. "Oh no!"

A small cloud of makeup powder-puffed up from beneath them as a rolling lipstick assaulted Dan's loafer. To this day, he'd never understood the mysteries of a woman's bag.

"Here, let me," he began.

"No! I've got it!"

They bent simultaneously toward the mound of sprawled purse contents, nearly knocking heads. "I'm sorry!" he said, down on hands and knees to help her.

"My fault!"

A scent overtook him as cunning and fine as the most succulent desert flower. Dan looked up into bewitching brown eyes less than six inches away. Whatever was happening here, he had to put a halt to it. This was no sensible way for a man pushing forty to behave. He was reeling like a raving teenager. He hadn't been in a position this compromising with a woman in a while, and it showed. All sorts of crazy thoughts went racing through his head, like how it might feel to kiss her good and hard as she probably deserved.

"You guys okay over there?" a pair of cowgirl boots called from the corner.

"Thanks, we've got it!" Gwen replied, scooting back on her knees. She couldn't believe this mess! What had she gotten herself into? Here she was with this hunky beast of a man, trapped beneath a solid yet decorative desk.

He had a rugged face, tanned like he was used to working outdoors. His sandy hair held a hint of sunlight too. Toned muscles strained beneath his suit jacket as he posed on all fours, looking far more like a predator in the wild than a staid art collector. Gwen had an improbable instinct to flee but was powerless to run away. He'd been an impossible man above board, but down here in the shadows, he revealed something more. Instinct told Gwen that Holbrook was the sort of man who knew how to kiss a woman and kiss her right. She imagined getting swept into his powerful arms, his mouth moving down on hers...

"Are you all right?" His gaze dove into her as heat crept up her cheeks.

"Yes, fine. That's all, I think," she said, scooping the remainders into her clutch.

Gwen didn't know why his gorgeous stare had unnerved her so. It wasn't like she was attracted to him, for heaven's sake. If her take on Holbrook was correct, he had plenty of women falling all over him already. What would a sophisticated Western entrepreneur like him want with a Carolina girl like her anyway? Apart from a quick good time, probably not a lot, and Gwendolyn Marsh was quite done with being somebody's goodtime girl, thank you very much.

Little lines pulled at the corners of his mouth, and she realized suddenly they were still both on the floor. "If you've got all you need, don't you think we should..." He gave a thumbs-up, and she pushed back, standing awkwardly.

Holbrook brushed off his trousers, the slight tugs showing off powerfully muscled thighs. Clearly not just a gallery owner, she thought, cheeks flaming as he caught her staring.

A tense moment ensued as both appeared to forget where they were or what they were there for. As if to remind them, the California man loudly cleared his throat.

"Just finishing up," Dan told him. "Ms. Marsh," he began, addressing her.

"Gwen, please. I'd be happy if you called me Gwen." She smoothed the wrinkles from her dress and straightened the neckline.

"Gwen," he said, offering up his first true smile since she'd arrived, and boy, was it a winner. If a heartbreaker contest existed in all of the Southwest, Gwen would bet on Holbrook to take the prize. "I'm afraid I've already taken up too much of your time."

Gwen spied the California couple circling closer like sharks, apparently having grown tired of waiting, and panic set in. What a terrible two days she'd had. First, her flight to Atlanta was delayed. Then, she'd missed her Albuquerque connection, causing her to miss her originally scheduled gallery appointment. To top it off, when she finally got a replacement flight, she'd chipped a nail stuffing her bulging carry-on into the overhead compartment.

Making Santa Fe from the airport last night was easy. Finding the craftily concealed entity of Holbrook and Holstein on Canyon Road this morning proved more elusive. Even her GPS was miffed, telling her to make legal U-turns wherever possible, no matter that the prospect involved going round and round in the Vegan Market parking lot.

Now, after making a wreck of this business call, she'd be leaving here having done no business at all. Not one sale to the gallery, despite her tumultuous flight and anxiety-producing encounter with Dan Holbrook.

Gwen pulled herself up a little straighter and squared her small shoulders. She couldn't leave New Mexico without getting what she came for. Too many people depended on her, and this was the one shot she had.

"Maybe we can continue this conversation later?" she asked with a hopeful twist to her lips.

"I was just about to suggest that."

"You were?" she asked with surprise.

"Ms. Marsh…" He stopped himself. "Gwen… Do you really think Holbrook and Holstein would have had you come all this way if we didn't have a genuine interest in your work?" Crinkles formed at the corners of his blue eyes, and Gwen's heart soared.

"But I thought you said the prices quoted to me in the email were…"

"Everything in life is negotiable. Well, almost everything. Tell you what, why don't you give me a few hours to put through a phone call to France, and I'll see what I can do."

In an instant, Gwen retracted every uncharitable thought she'd had about him. When she'd first walked into the swanky, upscale warehouse and spied him double-checking the pricing on a large wall weaving, she'd imagined him incredibly stuck-up. Who wouldn't be with that six-foot build and well-proportioned frame that spoke of power and unerring self-control? She'd pegged him as the rigid sort who never took no for an answer and considered his own words the final determinant. Now that he was showing a small sliver of humanity, she realized she might have misjudged him.

"I'd love to talk again," she said, meaning it sincerely. "When's best for you?"

"How about tomorrow at lunch? Will that work?"

Ms. Holstein, his business partner, Gwen presumed, had proposed that Gwen make a little vacation out of her stay in Santa Fe while she was at it. Her sister Marian had thought it was a fine idea too. *"Go for it, Gwen! Now's your chance to finally get away!"* What Marian didn't know, and Gwen hadn't been prepared to tell her, was that Gwen's coming to Santa Fe had a whole lot to do with her.

"I'm booked at the inn for ten days," she said, smiling softly. "So, lunch tomorrow is fine."

Holbrook surprised her with a smile of his own. "Awesome." He nabbed a gallery card and quickly penned something on the back. "Let's meet here. Something tells me the conversation might flow a little better between us given a couple of avocado margaritas."

"Avocado?" she retorted, half stunned, half horrified.

Holbrook gave a genuine chuckle as she accepted his card. "Nobody's forcing the hard stuff on you. I'm sure there will be tea and soda available too."

There was a twinkle in his eye that set her tailbone tingling. Slow down there, sister, Gwen told herself. This is strictly business now. Not anywhere near a date.

"What time?" she asked primly, pinning her clutch to her side.

He studied her in an amused way. "One o'clock okay?"

"One sounds fine!" she said, scurrying toward the exit before she could do or say something absurd.

"Watch the…!"

Gwen spun toward him, noting she'd nearly upset a pretty, handblown glass vase with the edge of her bag. She grimaced, slinking out the door as the gaping Californians gawked on.

Once outside and beyond sight of the gallery's windows, Gwen snatched her bag from beneath her arm and whacked herself soundly on the forehead. Stupid, stupid, stupid. She might have blown the whole thing. And not just by breaking a priceless piece of art. The way she'd started things out had been nothing short of shameless. Crafting a confrontation with the primary gallery owner. Clearly, that could lead to nothing but butting heads.

Gwen felt a warmth surge through her, recalling their close encounter of the nearly carnal kind. There was more to Dan Holbrook than met the eye. Hadn't he just proved that with his turn of kindness at the end? But the truth of the matter was that whatever sort of man he was, or wasn't, was beside the point. Gwen had come to Santa Fe on a mission, and that mission involved dollar signs. She didn't just want the money; she needed it. Twenty thousand in cash, and she wasn't leaving New Mexico without it.

Dan finished business quickly with the couple from Los Angeles after offering sincere apologies for making them wait. They'd prearranged to purchase the desert photo series, and everything, including price negotiations, thank goodness, had been settled with Nancy in advance. It was a simple matter of the pair presenting a check and Dan providing the receipt. In the morning, he'd arrange for shipping, and Nancy's gallery assistant would be in to help with the details. That would be the simple part of Dan's day. Lunchtime could prove more problematic.

Dan chided himself for suggesting Gwen meet him at La Cantina rather than here. Outwardly, he told himself that he was being charitable. Gwen had seemed so uptight at the gallery, perhaps a more comfortable venue would be less intimidating. He'd read her résumé and understood that if she sold through Holbrook and Holstein, it would be her first real sale, her official launch in the art world. But deep in the veiled recesses of his soul, Dan suspected a slight ulterior motive. He hadn't enjoyed the company of an attractive woman in ages, and this was a safe way to do it. Lunch in the middle of the day, a straightforward business deal? What could be more innocent? Raw doubts niggled at him as he warned himself against getting in too deep. The way he'd sprung the invitation on Gwen had been completely out of character. It had been a split-second decision, an act on impulse, and Dan was anything but an impulsive man.

He would never have built his empire of custom-design homes for the moneyed set if he'd operated from a basis of anything but collected cool. In those circles, Dan was known for his keen eye and level head, as well as his effectiveness in putting together a team. From the highest-level architect to the most basic yet very skilled carpenter, every one of Holbrook Designs' workers was treated with utmost respect and handsomely paid. This was particularly appreciated in the current economic climate but had always been the operational mode for Dan. Whether times were easy or hard, Dan's business remained steady. While his homes certainly weren't cheap, they were of a consistent quality the buyer could count on. Plus, Dan was a man of his word who stood by his product. People could depend on him to deliver the best and ensure they had a comfortable and stunningly beautiful place in which to live for years to come. It was an area in which Dan felt confident, competent.

This temporary gallery-running made him feel something altogether different, and Dan didn't like it one bit. While working with the California couple had gone fine, dealing with Ms. Gwendolyn Marsh had thrown him unexpectedly off-kilter. Nancy had nowhere near prepared him for that. Just because he'd helped his big sister finance this place, that didn't mean he wanted to be involved in any intimate way. Nancy was the art history major who loved the ins and outs of acquiring art. Running a gallery in Santa Fe had always been her dream, and once Dan had found himself in a position to help with that, he'd been more than happy to foot the bill. He'd never imagined that she'd repay him by listing his name as the primary gallery owner. This perpetually led to confusion, like during his exchange with Gwen today.

No matter. He'd straighten all that out tomorrow. Surely, after a good lunch and some cordial conversation, they'd arrive at a fair compromise on price. It would be a simple matter to smooth over during coffee and dessert. Then Ms. Gwendolyn Marsh could cart her sexy little tail all the way back to North Carolina, and Dan would continue counting down the days to Nancy's return, when he would once again be free to retreat to the peaceful quiet of Paradise Ranch. Life wasn't really so complicated after all, Dan decided, thinking it through. All you needed was a plan. And Dan's plans didn't include one firecracker of a Southern belle upending his world and sending his foolish heart racing. For Dan Holbrook, days like that were done. His throat ached at the memory. He swallowed hard, trying to force it back down. Dan had stepped into the fire once and had come out barbequed. No need to start poking at coals again.

Gwen sat on the patio of her airy suite, surrounded by sweeping adobe walls, potted ferns, and cactus flowers. Despite the record-high temperatures, the lack of humidity made it pleasant enough to stay outdoors in the shade. She sipped at her host's complimentary glass of chardonnay, knowing she needed to be cautious. At seven thousand feet above sea level, one glass of wine could feel like two. The inn's cocktail hour had also offered a selection of fruits, vegetables, and cheeses, and Gwen had fixed herself a small plate as a buffering against the booze. She'd have to remain mindful of herself tomorrow at lunch, particularly in light of the proposed margaritas.

Gwen couldn't help but feel a slight tingle of hopeful anticipation. For the first time in as long as she remembered, she'd be eating out with an eligible man. She knew, of course, that it was just an art deal, and she was merely passing through town. It was nonetheless hard to deny the tiniest fluttering in her tummy that sprang to life each time she recalled being face-to-face on the floor with the undeniably handsome Holbrook. Had something authentic actually passed between them, or had Gwen been so nervous and delusional as to have imagined the whole thing?

She glanced down at the simple gold band on her left ring finger. Gwen wasn't sure if it was her marriage she couldn't forget or her failure to maintain it. *"Marshes aren't quitters!"* her mom, Elizabeth, had always said. While life may have quit on Elizabeth, she wasn't about to let her daughters give up on anything. It was a mantra burned into them, her and her sister Marian both. Gwen only wished Marian had quit having babies about three children ago. Marian was expecting her sixth, and after years of verbal and physical abuse, her alcoholic husband, Tom, had finally run out on her. Gwen had truthfully considered this a blessing, as it had been clear after the first couple of years that Marian never intended to leave Tom.

Marian worked part-time as a hospital nurse and tried to get the day shift as much as possible. When she was gone, she left her oldest, the eleven-year-old, in charge. During night shifts, her elderly neighbor, Ms. Tilly, helped out. During the academic year, Marian had daycare arranged for the twins while the others were in school. She wasn't sure how she'd manage once the new baby came along, especially under the threat of losing her home. Marian's mortgage was several months overdue, and the collectors were moving in. She hadn't told Gwen that Tom stopped sending payments, or that she was in so deep, until it was almost too late. As it was, Marian barely had funds in her meager savings account to buy a few months' worth of diapers. Her checking account was essentially empty, being worn down month after month by her family's needs, including the kids' doctors' bills.

Marian had been in tears when she'd told Gwen the truth. If she lost her house, she feared her children would be taken away from her. She had nowhere else to go. Gwen's sparse two-bedroom could scarcely hold them all, not for any length of time, at least. And their mom, having long ago been placed in the memory-care unit of a retirement home, was far from being able to help. She barely scraped by on Social Security and most days didn't recognize either of her daughters, besides.

If Marian could just hang on one more year until the twins were in school, she thought she could make it. With only the new baby to place in daycare, she'd be able to work full-time. That would give her benefits like a retirement pension and health insurance. She'd be better able to meet her kids' medical expenses as well as plan for her own future. As it stood, she had six months of back mortgage to pay and another twelve months' obligation to look forward to. She was overwhelmed and in pieces, unsure of what to do. Taking Tom to court wasn't an option. Marian didn't have the financial resources, and even if she did, it would be hard squeezing blood from a stone. Tom was on and off the bottle and in and out of work. She couldn't rely on him now any more than she had during their marriage.

It was a dire and depressing situation. Gwen had thought for weeks about what she might do to help her sister. The trouble was Gwen was in financial strife herself. Robert had been so furious at her for kicking him out, he'd run up over ten thousand dollars in credit-card debt on purpose. The pro bono women's shelter attorney Gwen consulted said there was nothing Gwen could do about Robert maxing out the account jointly held in their names.

Gwen was unfortunately just as liable for half of his debts as entitled to half of his earnings. Good luck with that. Robert, a successful production assistant with a Hollywood company providing East Coast sets, had found plenty of loopholes in which to stash his cash. Gwen twisted the simple wedding band once, realizing her cheeks were damp.

She finished off her chardonnay, more determined than ever to sell those canvases and at the best possible price. She'd started small with a few local juried art shows around town, then had dared to put a modest portfolio of slides together and began sending it out. Holbrook and Holstein in Santa Fe had been her first real nibble. In effect, it had been a really big bite. Top dollar for her work, plus the cost of round-trip air tickets and accommodations to boot. Holbrook probably thought that Gwen was being greedy, trying to barter up the price for her own gain. Nothing could be further from the truth. Marian's kids needed their Mamá, and Gwen needed to help her baby sister. One way or another, Gwen was going to see this through. Dan Holbrook could think anything about her that he liked. She'd never see him again after tomorrow anyway.

Chapter Two

When Dan got to La Cantina, Gwen had already arrived. He spied her seated at a table for two in the large atrium styled like a Spanish courtyard and decorated in colorful tile. She studied the menu as he approached, a white peasant blouse sweeping her shoulders, hair pinned up in a casual way that offset her cheekbones and fair complexion. Dan had to stop walking and catch his breath. She was truly a beautiful woman, even more beautiful than he'd given her credit for yesterday at the gallery. Then again, yesterday at the gallery, she'd appeared primed to bite his head off. Today, she just looked hungry.

"Can I help you find a table, sir?" a tall waiter in a waistcoat inquired.

"Thanks, I see where I'm going," Dan said, shaking the reverie. Hearing their exchange, Gwen looked up at him and smiled. He felt a little twist in his gut and realized this was worse than he thought. Dan smiled back pleasantly, determined to pull himself together. He envisioned a large Weber grill, coals searing beneath its grate, and suddenly felt driven to thirst.

He joined Gwen at the table, exchanged pleasantries, then took a long drag of water from the glass that had been provided at his place. She eyed him curiously as he drained it all.

"It's murder out there," he said, referencing the weather.

"Certainly is hot," she agreed.

"I hope you found this place okay."

"Oh yes, just fine." Warm brown eyes sparkled enticingly.

"They've got some really great specials today. Have you taken a look?"

Gwen turned over the menu in her hands, and he wondered again about that wedding band. How long had she been divorced, and why would she continue to wear it? Dan reminded himself that delving into Gwen's personal affairs was none of his business.

She surveyed the ample list of entrees. "Any recommendations?"

"Depends on whether you like spicy."

She gave him a big, appealing grin. "I love spicy food. All kinds. But I'd love to try something particular to the region." Why did she have to look so darned likable today? She really wasn't cooperating in encouraging Dan to keep his distance.

"Would you like me to order for us?" he asked, wanting to be helpful yet not wishing to overstep his bounds.

"That would be nice. Thanks." Gwen lowered her face to her menu to disguise a faint blush.

Dan fought a swell of heat, surmising there wasn't enough air in here. "Okay, be honest with me. Yes or no to avocado margaritas?"

"You weren't kidding, were you?" she asked with surprise.

"I may be many things, but I'm not really much of a kidder."

She stared at him intently, trying to read him. Dan tried to repress a smile but felt his eyes crinkle just the same.

"That was kidding, wasn't it?" she asked, waving a scolding finger.

He let loose a belly laugh, enjoying himself. "I'm afraid it was."

Gwen released a tiny puff of air, apparently relieved. "I'll try an avocado margarita," she answered, "but just one."

A little while later, Gwen took her first taste of the tantalizing southwestern treat. Finely pureed like a smoothie, it was silky, cool, and delicious. You couldn't taste the tequila at all. Gwen was glad she'd made the advance decision to stick with one. Holbrook did too. He ordered them a delicious chicken poblano over Mexican rice, with a cold gazpacho soup to start. It was a perfect meal, and he had been right. After a couple of margaritas, their conversation flowed a lot more smoothly. For one thing, she learned that while his name was on it, he didn't actually run the gallery. He was merely filling in this month for his older sister Nancy. His real work involved home building of some kind. It was a job he seemed to enjoy and which often kept him outdoors.

"I insist that you call me Dan," he said as their plates were cleared. "Mr. Holbrook hardly seems right with me calling you Gwen. You're making me feel like an old man."

"Oh, I suspect you're not that old," she said, feeling as if she was flirting.

He colored slightly around his open collar. "Thirty-nine next month. Practically over the hill."

He was dressed casually today, in khaki slacks and an azure polo shirt that complemented his eyes. The shirt fit him nicely, stretching evenly across his broad and muscled chest. Gwen found herself wondering what it would be like to press her hands against it, feel the strength and power there. Maybe that margarita was getting to her after all.

"Well, I'm thirty-two, so not that far behind you."

He took a long, slow sip of his drink, surveying her over the rim of his glass. "Something tells me it will be some time before Ms. Gwendolyn Marsh makes it over that hill."

Now was he flirting with her? The way he studied her made Gwen think Dan had more than painting on his mind. She imagined removing his shirt and applying a deep massage oil, stroking the musculature there. Heat welled within her, sending electric currents from her fingertips to her toes. Gwen reminded herself to stay on track. Maybe the margarita was getting to him as well. Although that seemed difficult to believe, given his sturdy and scrumptious build. Oh dear, there she went again. It was a relief when Dan changed the subject by suggesting dessert. Anything to take her mind off further explorations of that come-hither chest.

"It was a wonderful lunch, but I honestly don't have room for more."

"Not even jalapeño custard pie?" Dan tempted. Gwen had the sense that Dan Holbrook could tempt even the most sensible woman into almost anything.

"Maybe next time," she said, combating a new rush of heat with a long drink of water, which, instead of hitting her lips, splashed in her lap. "Oh dear!" Gwen brought her palms to her cheeks as Dan sprang from his chair.

"Take mine," he said, pressing his cloth napkin to her skirt. Suddenly, his warmth spread through her nether regions. She gasped, and he glanced up, their eyes locking.

"I'll get it, thanks," she stammered as he pulled his napkin aside, and she took to the task with hers, promptly dropping her napkin on the floor. "My goodness."

Dan scooped low to retrieve the soggy rag. He hesitated briefly to study her dangling ankle bracelet, then righted himself slowly, his sky-blue gaze grazing hers.

Dan reddened as he handed Gwen back her napkin. "I'll call the waiter over and ask for more."

"Don't bother," she said sweetly. "I think that's got it."

Gwen couldn't believe what a klutz she'd been. What was it about this man that made her all butterfingered? Okay, the truth was Marian had sometimes accused her of being a teensy bit clumsy, but she'd never been an out-and-out wrecking ball like this. It was probably a combination of things. Her mission for money complicated by Dan's inexcusable hotness. She found herself wishing briefly that his sister Nancy had been here to meet with her instead. A split-second later, she realized that was a lie.

The hard fact was Gwen was attracted to Dan. Seriously attracted. And perhaps he'd given indications that he was the slightest bit interested in her as well. But what was wrong with that? Colleagues could enjoy a simple flirtation, for heaven's sake. Gwen was sure it happened all the time. That certainly didn't mean it had to go anywhere. Gwen hadn't come to Santa Fe to find a man. She'd come to launch her art career and help her sister. Over time, she'd also be helping herself. After a while, she could do less and less of her day job and more of what gave her pleasure and caused her spirit to soar.

"You know," Dan said as coffee arrived for the two of them. "I've gone on at length about my work, and you haven't really talked about yours. Have you been painting long?"

"I did a bit in high school, but then sort of let it go."

"How's that?" he asked.

"When I started applying to colleges, my mom encouraged me to pursue something a bit more practical." She shrugged, resigned. "She may have had a point. I'm not sure what sort of job I might have gotten as an art major. I couldn't imagine teaching something I loved so much and found so personal. I'm afraid it would have taken the passion out of it for me. So I decided to finish in music instead."

"Music?" he asked with surprise. "Are you talented?"

"Not in the least," she said with a laugh. "In fact, do you know that expression?"

Dan grinned. "Those who can, do; those who can't, teach?"

"Precisely. I can't carry a tune in a bucket, and I'm impossibly inept on the keyboard."

Dan leaned forward on his elbows. "Then how…?"

"Oh, I have a great ear for things. I mean, when someone else is doing the playing, I can pluck the mistakes right out. Not that I'm hard on my students. I'm really a very encouraging teacher." And she was too. The children appeared to love her, and their parents praised her abilities. Gwen was just thankful that none of them had borne witness to her botchery of university piano recitals. It was a blessing that she could graduate in teaching without having to prove her own exceptional skill.

Dan gave a delighted chuckle. "What grades do you teach?"

"Elementary during the school year. In the summertime, I take private piano students on, all ages up to adults."

"So you could teach me?" he asked invitingly. Uh-oh, there he went, flirting again. Gwen doubted very seriously that she could teach the dangerously capable Dan Holbrook anything. At thirty-eight, he was bound to have seen a bit of the world and more than his share of women. Gwen reminded herself not to be foolishly flattered by his probably practiced attentions.

"I'm not sure about that. Something tells me you might not be the most cooperative student."

Dan raised his brows in surprise, then released another belly laugh. "You've probably got me there. Nancy tried to teach me 'Chopsticks' once when I was ten, and I never quite got through it."

Gwen couldn't help but soften at his self-effacing honesty. If she wasn't careful, she was going to start liking the man, and that might cloud her judgment in any business dealings. She finished her coffee, realizing lunch was nearly over and they'd not yet talked turkey.

"Some people have more natural talent than others," she said kindly.

"Like you do for painting, for instance," he said, turning the conversation in what Gwen hoped would be the right direction.

"I appreciate you thinking so," she said, feeling her heart warm. "I really enjoy what I do. The thought that it might also bring happiness to someone else is just wonderful."

"When did you start painting again?"

"Oh, I did it off and on. Just for me, you know. Could never entirely let it go over the years. Then on my thirtieth birthday, my little sister, Marian, gave me the most beautiful gift, a completely new set of oils and brushes. I'd been getting by with old things, mostly cast-offs from the school art teacher who'd been sympathetic to my cause."

"Marian must know you very well."

"We're super close," Gwen said, feeling the burn in her throat. "The gift was extra special because oils are expensive, and Marian… Well, she…she doesn't have a lot of money."

"So that's when it really started? When you began painting more regularly?"

Gwen nodded, willing away the unpleasant memory of Robert coming in and upending her very first seascape. *"Ridiculous,"* he'd said. *"Where do you think you'll get with that? You sure as hell can't sing. What makes you think you can paint?"*

Gwen blinked, briefly turning away. When she turned back to Dan, she found herself caught up in his sky-blue gaze. The way he looked at her was soothing, as if he had all the time in the world to listen to what she had to say, and like none of it was ridiculous.

"I did start painting more then, yes. It was easier without the resistance."

"Resistance?"

"That doesn't really matter anymore," she said, forcing a smile. "I found a way to move beyond it."

"And the clients at Holbrook and Holstein will be glad. I assure you."

"I'm glad you brought that up so I didn't have to."

He looked at her earnestly. "Gwen, I've had a great time at lunch with you, really I have. But I have no illusions about why a beautiful young woman like you would spend time with a washed-up old bachelor like me."

Gwen blushed at the compliment but wasn't about to let herself get derailed by his manly attentions. As long as he'd started the ball rolling, she needed to push it along. "You underestimate yourself, Dan. But it's good to know you've reconsidered underestimating my work."

His gaze filled with admiration. She was being a little saucy, and he apparently liked it. "I spoke with Nancy like I promised. Holbrook and Holstein is prepared to set a fair price for your art. We can't quite go up to four thousand, but if you're willing to agree to three-five, we think we can cut a deal."

The way he'd said that made it almost seem real, as if this was actually going to happen for her. Gwen tried to contain her excitement. "Excellent," she said, giving him what she hoped was a warm, even smile. "I'm open to discussing that."

"Of course, I'm sure you're familiar with how things work," he continued. "Gallery sales are commission based, so whatever price we arrive at is provisional."

The corners of Gwen's mouth took a downturn. The fact was, she didn't know this at all. "I'm sorry. I'm not sure what you're saying."

Dan set his empty coffee cup aside and laced his fingers together in a sincere fashion. "I'm saying the gallery takes a commission. That's how it stays in business. Your work for sale there is basically on consignment."

The shock and horror hit her in the stomach like a sucker punch. "Consignment? But nothing in Ms. Holstein's email said anything about—"

His gaze softened, genuinely apologetic. "I'm sorry, Gwen. She probably thought you knew. Most of the artists we deal with are...experienced."

Gwen felt a flash of anger, but she quelled it, realizing nobody had intentionally tried to mislead her. "Are you saying I won't be getting any money now?" she asked, trying to mask the desperation in her voice.

"Now?" he asked, as if he'd never considered the possibility. "You mean, like during your ten-day trip to Santa Fe?

"Gwen, we're dealing with a process, here. We agree on what we think a reasonable buyer might pay in this market. That is the sale price. The two of us sign a contract, and then you ship the canvases. Once they're here, we hang them up for sale. As money comes in, it's funneled directly to you, less the gallery's twenty-percent commission."

Gwen felt her entire world crumbling in on her. Maybe it was her fault, hoping for too much in just one visit. But what if things didn't sell? What if enough money didn't come on time? What if the bank failed to extend its credit?

Gwen thought of Marian and her kids, of lives pulling apart... Of Robert's repeated infidelities... Her art box being tossed into the ocean... Something cut loose inside, and she felt like she might lose it at any second, break down sobbing on this already soppy napkin. She opened her purse and pulled out a tissue.

Dan reached a steadying hand across the table and laid it on hers. "Gwen? Are you all right?"

"Excuse me," she said, dabbing the corner of her eye. "I'll be right back."

Dan sat there for the longest time, wondering what he'd done wrong. Could Gwen truly have thought she'd fly out of here in just over a week with wads of cash lining her pockets? Were her circumstances really that bad? She'd seemed so fragile when she'd rushed out of here, as if she might break apart at any minute. Dan had no idea what sort of situation she was in, but he did know one thing. If he could, he wanted to help.

After what seemed like an eternity, Gwen resurfaced, all fresh-faced with newly applied lipstick and powder. Dan was finally starting to understand why women kept so much nonsense in their purses. It was for emergency situations like this.

"Any better?" he asked with concern.

She gave a sniff and lifted her chin.

"Allergies. Never know when they're going to hit me."

"Glad you're okay."

"Yes," she said, taking her seat. "Just fine, thanks." She noted the credit card receipt on the table. "Oh, you've already paid the bill. I'm sorry. I didn't mean for you to—"

"My pleasure," he said, meaning it. He hadn't had a lunch this interesting with a woman in a decade. Everything he'd learned about Gwen had been fascinating. But what intrigued him most was all that he didn't know. "Gwen," he began, hoping to broach the subject lightly. "I couldn't help but notice you were a little…thrown by our arrangement."

"The consignment, you mean?" she asked proudly. "Oh no, I knew all about it. I suspected that's how things went." It was a brave cover, but Dan saw straight through it. Didn't help her that her chin still trembled slightly.

"That's how it normally goes," he answered. "But there's really no need for us to go getting all bogged down in normalcy, wouldn't you say?"

She knitted her delicately sculpted brow. "I'm sorry? I'm not sure I follow."

A few gold tendrils broke free from their pins and spilled forward. Dan had an idiotic impulse to reach out and sweep them back, chancing a touch of her alabaster skin. He stopped himself just in time, tucking away the bill receipt in his pocket instead. "How soon can you get your canvases out here?"

"To Santa Fe? Why, in just a few days. They're all packaged and ready to ship."

"That settles it, then," he said with a wide, easy grin.

"Settles what? I haven't signed any contract."

"No, but if you will, I have an idea," he said slyly.

"What sort of idea is that?" she whispered, angling forward.

Dan looked straight in her eyes with calm reassurance. "We don't normally operate this fast, but I do have a list of potential buyers I can contact."

Her face lit up like the most stunning sunrise. "Are you saying what I think you are?"

"If fortune smiles on us, we might be able to sell a canvas or two before you leave."

"All five?" she asked with a hopeful glow.

Dan feared he'd done the wrong thing, caused her to think it was a certainty that this would go off. But when she'd gone all weepy on him, it had been impossible for Dan to stop himself. The truth was he had the means to buy all five of Gwen's canvases himself without even making a dent in his money-market account. But that would make the dealings between them personal, and Dan had vowed to keep things on a professional level.

Dan returned her gaze with cautious determination. "Let's not go pushing our luck," he said, sensing he'd gotten in over his head. He envisioned a huge, raw T-bone getting tossed onto a grill. Perspiration built at his brow, and he lifted Gwen's soggy napkin from the table to dab it.

"I need to get back to work," he said, standing and helping Gwen with her chair. "Think you might stop by later to sign the papers? The gallery closes at eight. That would be a good time."

"Eight o'clock it is," she said with a smile that knocked his socks off and held potential to knock other items of clothing off too.

Dan said a polite good-bye, then hustled out of there like a rabbit being hunted by a pack of wild coyotes. He needed to get his head together and figure his way through these next few days. Not that this should be a problem for a take-charge guy like him who knew how and where to draw the line.

Dan knew it was for the best, and really in Gwen's interest, for him to back off from any sort of romantic notions now, while the backing was good. No matter what

Santa Fean magazine said about Dan being the "Best Billionaire Bachelor Catch in the West," privately he knew his shortcomings would give even the most understanding woman pause. Dan had been down that dusty trail once and was determined never to go there again. Didn't matter what sort of attractive filly came out of the gate. The fact of the matter was Dan wasn't riding.

Chapter Three

Gwen left the restaurant by exiting onto the main plaza, an oasis of green in the earth-toned adobe town. Huge shade trees lined its crisscrossing sidewalks, dotted with wrought-iron benches and lampposts. Bordered by the nation's oldest public building, the Palace of Governors, on one side and an array of upscale shops on the others, it was the city's central gathering spot and playground, complete with a bandstand in which an impromptu flautist played. Gwen strode past a snow-cone vendor and a couple of quesadilla carts on her way to explore the smattering of handmade goods the locals had spread on the ground atop woven blankets. She surveyed the assorted silver jewelry, accented with turquoise, and small trinkets for sale with an appreciative eye, and made complimentary small talk with the Native American and Mexican peoples proudly showcasing their wares.

A warm breeze blew as the sun angled high, bathing Santa Fe in its rosy glow, the impressive Sangre de Cristo Mountains just visible in the distance, their highest peaks capped with snow, even in summertime. Gwen made her way up a side street to visit Saint Francis Cathedral, a stunning Romanesque Revival structure challenging the surrounding adobe architecture with its sweeping arches and brightly hued stained-glass windows.

Perspiration dampened her hairline as she climbed the steps to the building's entrance. It was warmer in the sunlight, the scarcely filtered ultraviolet rays bearing down on her, causing her feet and hands to swell. At once, the thin gold band on her left ring finger felt too tight. She twisted it slightly as she continued her ascent toward the cathedral's front door. Gwen hadn't prayed for anything in a long time. In fact, she hadn't been to church since Robert left. Maybe she should have. Thinking it over, she understood she had much to be thankful for. Not least among her blessings was her opportunity to come here.

Gwen passed through the enormous wooden door, her senses immediately engulfed by burning incense. Though she wasn't Catholic, she didn't believe God would mind if she took a spot on a pew for a few moments to mull through her life. What an event it had been. There'd been so much to it she'd never seen coming. When she met Robert in college, he'd appeared so promising. He was ambitious and fun and seemed poised to carve out a good life for himself and any lady lucky enough to join him. When he'd asked Gwen to marry him just before graduation, she'd been over the moon. He had a good job offer in Wilmington, and they could settle in the nearby town where Gwen had grown up and her family still lived. It had all seemed so idyllic at first.

Gwen glanced down at the completely ineffectual wedding ring as her hand rested in her lap. It hadn't taken long for Robert to find someone he thought more intelligent and interesting than her. She bored him to tears with her tales of kids in school and had no real talents as far as he could gather. The people he worked with were insightful, intuitive, interesting… Maybe if Gwen looked more at the papers or followed the news, she'd be interesting too, though he kind of doubted it.

Gwen heaved a sigh, knowing she couldn't continue to beat herself up over Robert's shortcomings. When she was thinking clearly, as Marian often encouraged her to do, she understood that her marriage falling apart had more to do with him than her. Or perhaps it was due to them both and the fact that, once they'd escaped from the cocoonlike sanctuary of the university, neither of them truly fit together. Gwen wondered sadly if she was destined to fit together with any man. Perhaps that wasn't in the cards for her, and maybe that was okay. If her art took off and she built herself a career, something that she adored and was really proud of, that might be enough.

She considered her meeting this evening with Dan, realizing she'd been acting like a silly schoolgirl. It wasn't his fault she hadn't dated since her divorce, so why should she hold him accountable for her surging hormones? Any nice-looking man who'd paid her attention would likely have made her feel the same. As an elementary schoolteacher, she simply hadn't had much opportunity for that. All the men she met were either married or formerly married and quickly reattached. It seemed the decent ones didn't last long on the market. From what she'd gathered from her quick perusals of Internet dating sites, the perpetual bachelors all seemed to have something wrong with them. Then again, Dan appeared normal. Exceedingly normal, healthy, and sexually enticing as well. So why hadn't a tamale-hot catch like him been snapped up already?

Gwen decided to head back to the inn to cool off for a few hours before her gallery appointment. This praying business didn't seem to be going too well. She thought she'd probably done it wrong. It had been such a while, she couldn't tell. In any case, she was grateful to Dan for granting her this chance. At the heart of it, Gwen understood that was all this really was, a chance to sell some of her art to a very fine place and hopefully help turn her sister's life around. That was worth a few amens, no doubt. She dipped her head, offering them quickly, and bowed out of the cathedral before anyone could stop her and ask her for money. That was one part of going to church she hadn't forgotten. There was a lady near the door collecting donations for the restoration fund. Gwen slipped silently past her and out into the sunshine before the woman could hold up a brochure. Maybe once Gwen was rich and famous she'd feel a bit more philanthropic. At the moment, she scarcely had cash for dinner. She'd have to hurry to catch the wine-and-cheese hour before the other guests cleaned out the Havarti.

Dan paced the redwood-pine floors, double-checking the time on his BlackBerry. The afternoon couldn't have dragged out more if he'd planned it. It all seemed to go in slow motion, as if he were deep-sea diving, arms and legs battling against ocean pressure.

The occasional browsers stopped by, and there was the shipment to get out to Los Angeles, but Nancy's assistant Megan had come in to see to that. She wore a nose piercing and a puckish haircut that added to her image of a small sprite sprinting around the gallery. Dan had never seen a twenty-three-year-old with so much energy. She was very astute though, her nimble mind eager to acquire anything and everything about gallery running. She hoped to manage a place of her own one day and apparently did some sort of printmaking on the side.

"That's it, then," Megan said, peering up at him through heavily mascaraed eyes. "Think that I might sneak out early? I've got a date for drinks at Nines." Nines was the hipster bar on an adobe rooftop overlooking the mountains.

"Don't let me hold you back," Dan said.

"Are you all right?" Megan asked. "You've seemed a little…off this afternoon. Maybe you should head out early too."

Dan was more than a little off; he was distractingly discombobulated. He'd spent over three hours poring through Nancy's customary client list, trying to discern those who might be interested in Gwen's work. If he'd had his head on straight, the task might have taken him forty-five minutes. Instead, he'd caught himself daydreaming at every turn, reliving his lively lunch with Ms. Gwendolyn Marsh. Just as in the gallery the day before, he'd been sucked in by the feminine scent of her. Didn't help one iota that she obviously perfumed her legs, legs that were attached to one knock-out of a womanly body, teamed with a damnably adorable and kissable, he couldn't help but reason, face. And, when her eyes sparked with delight at the thought that he might help her, could actually sell her canvases in this absurd ten-day timeframe, Dan's heart had done an unexpected flip-flop.

"I'm fine," he lied to Megan. "Why don't you go on ahead? I've got an artist stopping by at closing. I'll lock up."

Megan grabbed her colorful straw bag that looked large enough to hold a weekend wardrobe and pranced out the door.

Dan strode to the desk and withdrew Gwen's contract from the nearby filing cabinet. He glanced through the folder for maybe the tenth time today, ensuring everything was in order. The paperwork was all lined up. Now all Dan had to do was steel his heart. He was getting far too carried away with this. Just because Gwen looked like an angel and spoke in a sweet Southern twang that was sexy as sin, that didn't mean he'd have to give in to her. He was a rational man, by all accounts, savvy at business dealings and skilled at keeping his emotions in check.

Okay, he'd made that one mistake. But it wasn't like it was going to come back to haunt him. It had been more than a month now, and he'd heard nothing further about it. It had been a harsh lesson in letting sleeping dogs lie. Once you make a pact to move on, there should be no looking back. Looking ahead wasn't sounding so safe at the moment either. Gwen was scheduled to be in town only ten days. She had her life back East to lead, and Dan had his own ghosts to contend with here. He shook off a gloomy feel, determined to make the best of their meeting. Dan was sensible enough to know he could assist a damsel in distress without falling into bed with her. And just to make certain he hadn't forgotten, the fates had pressed a branding iron to his chest a mere six weeks ago to drive that message home.

Gwen tugged at the zipper of her skirt, sliding it up her ample hip. She'd put on a few pounds since her divorce but still looked okay, she supposed. She'd never been accused of being overly thin. Marian was the slight one in the family, while Gwen fought the perpetual battle of the booty. Breasts, hips, and thighs had a will of their own. No matter how she tried, they relished maintaining their prefab form. After a while, Gwen had just given up and decided to enjoy life. As long as she operated within reason, didn't diet or exercise too much, she could stay within the same five-pound range that she'd grown accustomed to and certain men seemed to appreciate.

Gwen flushed at the memory of Dan's sky-blue gaze. At first she'd thought he'd just been flattering her, trying to put a gallery contact at ease. But the more she pondered it, the less she thought so. As they'd sat there discussing canvas pricing, his heated perusal had washed all over her like the clearest Caribbean wave. Gwen imagined the two of them on a distant beach, Dan bare-chested in the sun. He'd tell her once more how beautiful she was, and, half-

176 How to Marry a Matador

naked in her tummy-control swimsuit, she'd feel forced to believe it. He'd take her by the waist then, pull her soft body to his, taut stomach muscles tensing as he wrapped his arms around her... Gwen heard the surf crash, water swirling furiously at their feet, as he brought his glorious mouth to hers.

Suddenly, she realized she'd stalled in applying her lipstick and was standing there all puckered up like a ridiculous guppy. "That's the price I pay for that second Shiraz," she scolded herself, vowing to make coffee. She was glad the suite's miniature kitchen supplied what she needed for that. Now where was the sugar cube she could find to quell her outlandish fantasies?

Gwen had considered putting on a flirty dress for her meeting with Dan tonight but now worried that might send the wrong message. She wasn't seeing him for any sort of social reasons, she reminded herself. They were convening to sign a contract, for heaven's sake. Gwen lifted her perfume bottle and spritzed her neck, wrists, and the backs of her knees with its fine aroma.

Gwen's belly warmed as she recalled how Dan had hesitated by her foot just an instant too long in retrieving her dropped napkin. If he'd touched her then, even by accidentally brushing her calf, she would have fainted. They would have had to call in the rescue squad to scoop her limp form off the New Mexican tile. It didn't take an expert to see the super-studly Dan Holbrook held more masculinity in one pinkie than the pallid and self-possessed Robert contained from head to toe.

Coffee, Gwen reminded herself, noting by the clock on the nightstand it was almost time. The sooner she got this over and done with, the better. If she could negotiate the paperwork without chancing to shake Dan's hand, all the better. Even after the coffee, Gwen didn't trust herself to touch him. This was what Marian called an unwelcome consequence of celibacy.

Gwen adjusted her bra, shifting her bosom into its proper place, then, quite as an afterthought, she was sure, gave her cleavage the tiniest little burst of Midnight Jasmine perfume.

Dan looked up as the door chime sounded. There she stood, looking as gorgeous as a desert sunset, the colors of her sexy, short dress swirling about her in mauve, gold, and russet browns. "Are you ready for me?" she asked, dark eyes sparkling with anticipation.

Dan thought he was, in fact had prepared for her all afternoon, but now he felt as awkward and uncertain as a teenager. "Of course," he said, working to get the words out in a businesslike manner. "Come on in." Her womanly scent overtook him as his eyes trailed from her ankles to her cleavage to her faintly colored cheekbones. "Please, have a seat." He indicated a spot, nearly missing his own chair. Dan scooted onto it as she pulled hers in toward the desk just a tad too close. The sweet angles of her knees pressed into his ever so slightly.

A crimson blush warmed her shoulders and swept up her delicate throat. "Oh! Oh my goodness. I'm so sorry!" she cried, backing up.

"No worries! Really," he protested.

Gwen sat up a little straighter in her chair and crossed her legs as Dan opened the file in front of him. He passed her the paperwork with an appreciative gaze.

"You look lovely tonight," he said, unable to stop himself.

Gwen met his eyes, her cheeks still aglow. "Thank you. You look…really super too."

Dan reined himself in, applying his best businesslike tone. "I believe everything's in order there," he said as she fanned through the pages. "If you'd like to look it over, I can answer any questions."

The sun dipped low outside, casting a tangerine hue throughout the wide-open spaces of the gallery as Gwen sorted through the agreement. After a few moments of studied concentration, she addressed Dan with a relieved smile. "It all seems straightforward." She'd worried it might be complicated, filled with legalese and fine-print sections. On the contrary, it basically laid out what they had discussed at lunch, with a few boilerplate clauses she supposed were included in most contracts of this kind. "Where do I sign?"

Dan indicated the line, then added his own signature to the page.

"Have you come up with any contacts? I mean, people who might buy my art?"

Dan smiled indulgently. "Don't you think we ought to get it here first?"

"Right! I'll have Marian send it out tomorrow. Like I said, it's all boxed and ready to go. All she has to do is call for shipping."

Dan wrote some numbers on a small notepad on the desk. "This is our account number for Southwest Express. Have your sister call this phone number and bill it to us. She can let them know where and when to pick up the packages."

"Well, thanks, that's very gracious. That will help a lot." Gwen couldn't let him know that her wallet was paper-thin or that her sister was destitute.

"I've actually already sent out a couple of emails, feelers, if you will, to gallery contacts who might have an interest in an East Coast ocean scene or two."

Gwen felt her face warm with excitement. "That's wonderful!" She fought an urge to race around the desk and hug him.

"As soon as the pieces arrive," he continued, "I'll start making follow-up calls. I'm hoping to have some serious buyers in looking by the end of the week. Assuming the shipment goes as planned."

Gwen sprang from her seat and lunged for his hand. "I don't know how to thank you," she said, taking his hand in hers and holding it firmly.

His gaze wrapped around her, trapping her in his heat. "It's my pleasure, really," he said, exerting delicate pressure against her palm. Little tingles raced up Gwen's arm, and instantly she knew she'd made a mistake. She'd told herself to keep her distance. Now, all she wanted to do was get closer still. Gwen released his grip, attempting to steady herself on wobbly knees. If merely shaking hands had this much effect, she'd hate to see the pool of putty she'd be in if he'd dared to kiss her.

"Have you eaten anything since lunch?" he asked with concern.

Gwen pulled herself together, realizing she must have suddenly paled. "I had some wine and cheese back at the inn."

"Havarti?" he asked, with uncanny insight.

"How did you…?"

He repressed a grin, pointing to the back of her head. Gwen ran panicked fingers through her hair, finding a nice little chunk of cheese caught up in her curls.

She stared at him, mortified. "I'm so embarrassed," she began.

"Don't be," he offered kindly. "I get Camembert in mine all the time."

She scanned his face for the hint of a smile but couldn't detect one beneath his deadpan.

"This time, I know you're teasing," she said, and the moment between them lightened.

Small lines tugged at the corners of his mouth as blue eyes crinkled. "Something tells me you're getting to know me too well." His gaze held a hint of longing mixed with caution. "Wine and cheese isn't much of a dinner. I know a place with great steaks, if you'd like to join me?"

Gwen knew she was wrong to say yes. Everything inside her screamed *caution, slippery roads ahead*. But all Gwen wanted to do was get in that spectacular sports car and drive.

"I'd love to," she said, accepting his invitation.

Dan led them down a side street to an elegant outdoor restaurant set a few blocks from the plaza. The shaded pathway to its entrance bypassed the abutting Loretto Chapel, a notable nineteenth-century structure in Gothic Revival style, complete with buttresses and spires.

"Have you been in there?" Dan asked as they strolled by the wind art adorning the chapel's lawn.

Gwen admired the huge hands of the whimsical brass structures cupping and turning in the breeze as the sun sank low. "Not yet."

Her view panned to a fanciful wood carving of a man guarding the chapel door.

"Saint Joseph," Dan said, indicating the statue. "I'll tell you the story over dinner. You do believe in miracles?" He was smiling at her in a playful way.

A shiver shimmied down Gwen's spine, as she thought it was nothing short of miraculous that she was here, right now, with him. Dan Holbrook was not just a feast for the eyes, he was funny and kind and apparently enjoying her company. Plus, he made her feel beautiful. Not just because he'd said it. It was in the way he looked at her, all the time.

"I'll keep an open mind," she said, smiling back at him.

Dan shoved his hand in his pocket to prevent himself from reaching out and taking hers. In some ways, it would have seemed natural as he led her toward the maître d. In others, it was completely absurd! Dan heaved a sigh, grateful good sense had prevailed.

"Are you all right?" she asked, chocolate-brown eyes imploring.

"Just taking in the evening," he said, thankful there was no wait for a table.

He ordered them filet mignon with a mushroom, red pepper, and sherry reduction, Caesar salads to start, and a choice bottle of Chilean red wine. Dan didn't want to mess this up. Gwen's dinner had to be perfect. He'd slipped the maître d an unseen tip to ensure it. He'd also told Gwen upfront that the meal was on him. He'd seen the way her brow had knitted slightly as she'd surveyed the menu prices. Dan wasn't sure what sort of money trouble she was in, but he could bet her budget didn't include places like this one.

"The service is fabulous here," Gwen said as her water glass magically refilled.

Dan had the impression Gwen wasn't used to men treating her right. He was glad to be able to change that, to show her that not all men were schmucks, maybe just the ones she'd previously run into. "Wait until you taste the food."

She smiled sweetly over the rim of her wineglass. "This carménère is delicious. I'm so glad I got to try it."

"Should go well with the steak," Dan said, hoping he'd scored a point. For the life of him, he wanted to impress this woman. She looked prettier than ever, sitting there relaxed in the candle's glow. He compared her now to how she'd appeared yesterday afternoon in the gallery, anxiously combative, like if he didn't see things her way, there'd be hell to pay. He probably liked this Gwen better. Though the truth of the matter was Dan didn't really mind the other one much at all. He could see a man getting used to a balanced measure of them both.

Dan took a sip of wine, knowing he was letting his emotions get the best of him. That was a dangerous mountain to climb when he understood what was on the other side: a clean downhill slide where his heart would take a tumble. Elena had been quite detailed in enumerating his faults.

A crescent moon rose as a smattering of stars poured onto the canvas of the night sky above them. Their salads arrived, artfully served and in a timely fashion.

"So, are you going to tell me the story?" she asked eagerly.

Dan was happy for the chance to take his mind off his gloomy thoughts. "Ah yes, the story of Loretto Chapel," he said, setting down his glass. He leaned forward on his elbows and lowered his voice. "And its mysterious spiral staircase."

"Staircase?" she asked with surprise.

"Legend has it the staircase in Loretto Chapel arrived as a miracle. Some to this day may dispute it, but many others do not."

"Go on," she pressed, intrigued.

"Rumor holds that when the chapel was completed in the eighteen hundreds, the dear nuns who lived there noted there was no staircase to get them to the choir loft on the upper level."

"Oh my!"

"So they prayed for nine days for a miracle. On the tenth day, an unknown carpenter appeared and offered to complete the task. He built the freestanding staircase all by himself without using glue, nails, or any central support. Then, as soon as he was done, the stranger disappeared just as mysteriously as he'd arrived, without ever having identified himself or demanding any payment. The good sisters of Loretto naturally took this as a miracle, and the man to have been Saint Joseph himself. The proof I believe lies in the number of steps of the freestanding structure, made of a wood not even found in this region."

"Well?" she asked, her eyes twinkling.

"Thirty-three. The age of Jesus Christ."

Gwen leaned back in her chair with a delighted laugh. "That's wonderful! What a fantastic story."

"It's not a story," he said with mock defensiveness. "It's a miracle." The corners of his mouth twitched slightly, and Gwen could tell he was repressing a smile. She was finally starting to read him, and for a girl who didn't like to read, that said a lot.

Gwen cocked an eyebrow and shot him an impish smile. "Do you believe in miracles, Dan?"

He captured her with his gaze, stilling her heart for a fraction of a second. "Let's just say I believe most things in life can be rationally explained."

"Most things don't mean all," she bantered lightly.

He raised his glass to hers as their salad plates were cleared and the entrées arrived. "You've got me there."

Everything smelled delicious. Gwen couldn't wait to dig in. She hadn't realized how hungry she'd gotten subsisting on complimentary inn food these past few days.

"How's your filet?" he asked as she took a heavenly bite that literally melted in her mouth. "Cooked all right?"

He was incredibly handsome in the soft light, flames from the outdoor fire caressing the solid lines of his face.

"Perfect. Everything's just perfect. I couldn't have had a better night."

"I'm glad," he said with a grin. "That just leaves tomorrow."

"What do you mean?"

"You've got a bit of time to kill while the shipment comes in. Got any plans?"

"I thought I'd take in an art museum or two."

"That sounds great. I've been considering taking the day off myself."

Gwen set down her fork. "Are you…asking me on a date?"

"You mean unlike this one," he deadpanned.

She gasped with surprise. "This was a date?"

"It could be if you wanted it to."

Gwen's heart went fluttering in all sorts of wild directions. Why on earth was he doing this? Surely there was no sense in it. She'd be gone by the week's end. "I'm not so sure that's a good idea."

"Which one?"

"This a date… Tomorrow. I…I don't know." And she didn't, she really didn't. She was feeling all jumbled up inside, like she'd desperately wanted something and now didn't know what to do once she'd gotten it.

"How about if we just call it an appointment, then? An arrangement between associates to go and see some art.

Besides," he added temptingly, "I know who serves the best chile rellenos in town."

It was patently unfair of him to play the food card. Gwen absolutely adored chile rellenos, almost as much as she was starting to adore this man. "It's a deal," she said, smiling broadly.

Dan walked Gwen back to the inn, night sounds singing around them. He'd really jumped in headlong with this one, but Dan couldn't completely blame himself. With her lovely looks and warm and charming personality, Gwen had led him right to it. He'd been having such a good time with her at dinner, he couldn't bear having the evening end. The only remedy for that was to suggest seeing her tomorrow. He didn't have much going on at the gallery, and what was left to do Megan could take care of.

Dan stole a glimpse of Gwen strolling beside him in the moonlight and wished for a moment that things weren't transitory. But they were, and he'd need to remain aware of that. Just because they'd planned to spend the day together didn't mean they'd have to become any more involved than they already were. He liked Gwen, dammit. She was sensitive and sweet, and he felt good when he was around her. Dan hadn't felt this good about himself in a very long while. He decided it was time.

They got to the exterior patio door of Gwen's private suite, and she opened her purse to withdraw the key, her cheeks still aflame.

"I had a really great time tonight," she said, beaming up at him and feeling very much as if it had been a date.

"Me too," he said, stepping a fraction of an inch closer. Sea-blue eyes washed over her, threatening to pull her under. And boy, did she want to get swept away. "I'm glad you agreed to see me tomorrow, even if it's just an arrangement."

Gwen sensed Dan could rearrange her heart every which way, if she wasn't careful. "I'm glad I'm seeing you too," she said, feeling the warmth in her cheeks.

"Ten o'clock work for you?" he asked, his tone growing gravelly.

"Uh-huh," she uttered, mesmerized by his gaze.

He moved nearer now, his mouth just inches away. "I'll be damned if I don't want to kiss you," he said, his voice a husky rasp.

And she'd be damned if she didn't want him to. "Dan..." she said, tilting up her chin and closing her eyes.

"But I won't," he said, snapping her back to attention, eyes open. "Not now. Not here. Not like this..."

She started to speak as he brought his fingers to her lips. "If ever I've seen a woman who deserves to be kissed well, it's you. But the timing has got to be right. You have to be sure." He cast a cursory glance at her wedding band and backed away. "I need to be sure. Something tells me we've both gone down a path neither of us wants to travel again."

Gwen's heart sank as her face burned hot. He was right, and she knew it. Neither of them could risk foolishly giving themselves away. It was only a kiss, but a kiss was often the beginning. She was old enough to know that, and Dan clearly was too.

Gwen couldn't guess who'd broken Dan's heart, but he'd obviously been hurt just as much as she had.

"Good night, Gwen," he said, shadows haunting his face.

She watched him turn and walk away, loneliness settling inside her like a large, heavy weight Gwen feared she'd never shake.

She let herself into her empty room and cried softly in the darkness, moonlight weeping in through slanted blinds. If only she'd found a man like Dan ten years ago, maybe neither of them would have had to live through these vestiges of pain. But the past was long ago and should be forgotten, Gwen thought, twisting the ring on her finger.

Perhaps meeting Dan now was a good thing, the right thing for them both. Maybe they were meant to be stepping stones, each of them strategically placed to help the other on to a better life. They could be friends, confidants even, during her short stay in Santa Fe. Maybe they'd each give the other someone to lean on, somebody who really understood, for the first time in a long time. That didn't mean they'd have to start falling in love.

Gwen sucked in a breath, praying it wasn't already too late. By the way her heart hammered against her chest, she wasn't sure.

End of excerpt from *Santa Fe Fortune.*

Ginny Baird thanks you for reading her work
and hopes to hear from you soon.

www.ingramcontent.com/pod-product-compliance
Lightning Source LLC
Chambersburg PA
CBHW030336180626
46810CB00003B/1382